HAPPY SANDS

Happy Sands Resort

Rat's Nest
(Ginny, Martin, Alistair, Ruby)

Eagle's Loft
(Dot, Ruthanne)

Beehive
(Mrs. Edwards, Esther)

Fish Bowl
(Dwayne)

Beaver Lodge
(Kathy, Tara, Todd)

Bear Den
(The Oliemens: Doug, Darla, and kids)

Squirrel Nook
(The Roccos: Ricky, Shelley, and kids)

CORNFLOWER
LAKE

UNIVERSITY OF CALGARY
Press

Happy Sands

Barb Howard

Brave & Brilliant Series

ISSN 2371-7238 (Print) ISSN 2371-7246 (Online)

University of Calgary Press
2500 University Drive NW
Calgary, Alberta
Canada T2N 1N4
press.ucalgary.ca

LIBRARY AND ARCHIVES CANADA CATALOGUING IN PUBLICATION

Title: Happy sands / Barb Howard.
Names: Howard, Barb, 1962- author.
Series: Brave & brilliant series ; no. 21
Description: Series statement: Brave & brilliant series ; no. 21
Identifiers: Canadiana (print) 20210133317 | Canadiana (ebook) 20210133325 |
  ISBN 9781773852164 (softcover) | ISBN 9781773852171 (PDF) | ISBN 9781773852188
  (EPUB)
Classification: LCC PS8565.O828 H36 2021 | DDC C813/.6—dc23

The University of Calgary Press acknowledges the support of the Government of
Alberta through the Alberta Media Fund for our publications. We acknowledge
the financial support of the Government of Canada. We acknowledge the financial
support of the Canada Council for the Arts for our publishing program.

Printed and bound in Canada by Marquis Book Printing
This book is printed on 70lb Opaque Smooth Cream paper

Editing by Aritha van Herk
Copyediting by Naomi K. Lewis
Cover image: Colourbox 42303281
Map images: Colourbox 43083326, 26463617, 25016706, and 26106739
Cover design, page design, and typesetting by Melina Cusano

For Mike

DAY 1

Call me Ginny. My real name is Ginette — but to me, that sounds like a too-small bottle of booze, the kind you used to get on airplanes. I'm a massage therapist. My forearms are tanks, not tankettes. If I use the right technique, I don't have to apply much pressure, but even light pressure, day after day, body after body, makes for a hearty forearm. I'm rounding the corner to twenty years in this profession; I'm good at it, and I've made a lot of people feel better. I even do massages during my annual summer vacation at Happy Sands. For the money, but also because I like helping people. Well, most people.

It's not only 'my' vacation at Happy Sands. It's also a holiday for my family. And, dare I say, it's even more of a holiday for them than for me. I mean, I do all the organizing and planning before we go, and also most of the work when we are there. But families need holidays. They create the nostalgic glue that holds us together for the rest of the year. And, at least if you believe the photos and advertisements, there is no better place to manufacture this glue than on the deck of a cute 1960s-style pre-fab cabin, overlooking a white sandy beach, under a perpetually sunny sky.

So here we are, en route to Happy Sands. Driving from Calgary to the Okanagan. From Cowtown to Peachtown. From gridded grey streets to curvy lakeshore drives. My husband, Martin, is beside me in the car. Right now, he's sleeping. He sleeps a lot, especially lately. In my usually-right opinion, he's depressed. To be fair, he still manages to get our family's laundry done every week.

Better than that, he does my work laundry, too — that's a lot of sheets. He even does our laundry at Happy Sands, which is a hassle, because there are no machines on site, so he has to drive to a laundromat to do it. But laundry isn't exercise. He'd feel better if he got more exercise. And if he got laid off from his downtown IT job. Martin tells everyone his dream is a Calgary-style layoff package, even though he knows those packages rarely happen anymore.

Of course, I haven't told Martin that he's depressed. At least, not directly. And if I were going to say something to him, it wouldn't be with our kids in the back seat. It might be during a beach walk, maybe after a rain so there's a gorgeous rainbow we are walking towards, and I could say something like: Marty, honey, could you suck it up like everyone else?

I glance in the rearview mirror. Sixteen-year-old Alistair is in the seat behind Martin. Eight-year-old Ruby is behind me. My portable massage table is folded and leaning up against the seat between them, a blockheaded third child.

It's close to lunchtime, so I turn into the Tim Hortons drive-thru in Sicamous. Martin leans towards me to read the drive-thru menu. His hair smells musty — like an old pillow. Because he spends so much time with his head on a pillow. Or maybe because he didn't have the energy to shower this morning. Or maybe because —

"I'll just have a coffee," he says.

"Have something to eat," I say. "You haven't eaten anything today." What I really want to say is that if he ate something, maybe he'd have enough energy to exercise. Or, if that's too much, maybe just enough energy to stay awake for the rest of the drive.

"I'll finish whatever Ruby orders," he says.

"Oh no you won't," Ruby says from the back seat. "I'm eating all of mine."

Ruby is notorious for ordering more than she can eat. She's competitive. Ordering a big meal and eating it all would be a win, to her way of thinking.

Alistair says, "Dad just wants a coffee. Why can't you just let him have a coffee?"

"He can have a coffee," I say. "Food was just a suggestion."

"I'll have a large box of Timbits," Alistair says. He squirms around a bit and adds, "This massage table is too big for the back seat."

I'd like to know where he thinks the massage table should go — it's too big for the trunk, and it's too expensive to be strapped on top of the car and exposed to the elements. And, also, I want to point out that Tim Hortons offers healthier options than a box of Timbits, but I let it go. I could eat a few Timbits myself.

From the pickup window, I hand Ruby her sandwich and juice. I place Martin's coffee in his outstretched hand and hope there's enough caffeine to fix his slump for the rest of the drive. Isn't it the job of the person riding shotgun to keep the driver awake with thought-provoking conversation sprinkled with flattering anecdotes from their mutual past? Not going to happen here. I hand Alistair his private box of forty Timbits. All in all, not the best lunch scenario, but not terrible. No need to start the summer holiday off with confrontations.

After Tim Hortons, near Vernon, Martin puts his hand on his stomach, winces dramatically. Oh, here we go, I think. He's going to complain about a stomachache like he always does around this point of the drive. I don't bother stating the obvious — that maybe he's had too much coffee and not enough food. Besides, Martin would reply that his stomachache is because I'm driving too fast. He always says that.

"Sore stomach? Would some water help?" I ask. As the unpaid holiday coordinator, I have supplied everyone with a bottle of water for the drive.

"Could you slow down a bit?" he says, then winces for emphasis.

Alistair announces that he also has a stomachache, and that it is definitely due to my 'speeding.' I don't say anything. It's not like either of them can see the speedometer. I'm pretty sure Alistair's stomachache is from scarfing back forty Timbits. And then Ruby pipes up that she doesn't have a stomachache, and that she has been in lots of cars going way faster than this. She claims all her friends' moms drive faster than me. I doubt it. Although I am impressed that Ruby doesn't have a stomachache — she did eat that whole sandwich, and she did it while reading a book in a moving car. Ruby reads books about dragons. One of the high points in my life was when she learned to read, because it meant I didn't have to read her any more dragon stories. The dragon genre is a real snooze for me.

We've been vacationing at Happy Sands since Alistair was a baby. Now here he is, moaning and complaining in the backseat — still kind of like a baby. A tall baby. He's built like a garden rake, so, despite his complaints about not having enough space, there is lots of room beside him for the massage table. I'll admit that his legs might be squashed — but he hasn't complained about them. Yet. His main gripe, other than his alleged stomach issue, is that he doesn't want to be on a family vacation at all. He believes he's old enough to stay at home alone. He tried to convince me that he is indispensable at his summer job, that he can't possibly miss a week of working the till at our local gas station. I didn't have the heart to tell him that as much as we'd all like to feel indispensable, there's usually another warm body that can easily replace us at our jobs. But I did remind him that he can't seem to make a meal without setting off the smoke alarm, and that played into the decision to keep him in our sights. And, I never said this to him, because I know it would be received with an eyeroll, but I imagine a day in the future when he will be an adult and living on his own, and this kind of vacation won't be in the cards anymore. In any event, a daily swim in a lake will motivate him to get back into swimming. Alistair quit his swim team last fall, said he was tired of getting up that early in the morning. But, hello, I was getting up and driving him to all that swim training, and I wasn't exhausted. Now he busies himself with his gas station job and lying around the house. I guess he is busy growing taller. Maybe that's exhausting.

Several hours later, when we turn off the highway and follow the gravel road into Happy Sands, Martin rolls down his window, lets in the hot dry Okanagan air. Plus a billow of dust. I look in the rearview mirror and see Alistair's eyes open, even though his head doesn't move. I hear Ruby close her book, lean forward to look out the front window. When we get to the Happy Sands entrance, she asks if she can be the first in our family to check out the beach. And see if anything has changed from last year. And find out if anyone has spotted the big old fish that the kids call Moby Trout. I stop the car and she is out in a second, running in her cutoffs and T-shirt. There is a red crease on the back of her thighs from the car upholstery, and one of her sneakers is undone.

In a surprise burst of energy, Martin yells out his window, "Do up your shoe!"

"I will!" she yells back, still running, shoelace flapping. So, this is our family entrance to Happy Sands for all to see and hear — Martin and Ruby yelling. Why not get a bullhorn and shout, hello everyone, the Calgary hillbillies have arrived.

"She's going to trip," Martin says. Pessimism is his strong suit.

"Maybe not," I say.

But she does trip, falls forward into the grass, protecting her face with her arms. Then she rolls onto her bum, ties her shoe, jumps up, and starts running again.

"Do you want to run to the beach with her?" I ask Alistair.

"No," he says.

"I thought it might be fun for the two of you."

"Nope."

I park behind our cabin, the one we always rent.

"Maybe we can unpack the car later," Martin says. "I'm beat."

"Yeah," Alistair says. "I hate the rush to get everything unloaded in, like, two seconds after we arrive."

"Sure. No rushing. We can unpack the car later." I say it all light and easygoing. But I think about the milk and groceries in the cooler since the morning, and that the temperature outside is 30°C, and for me, it will be a lot more relaxing to unpack now. Isn't that what most families do? And, I admit it, I wonder how Martin and Alistair got so worn out and rush-averse when I did all the packing and driving. Okay, okay, what I am really thinking, but in more colourful language, is that Alistair and Martin are a couple of useless jerks.

I unpack the car. No big deal. One duffel for each person, a few groceries, and a cooler. And now here I am. On the deck. Sitting in one of the four white plastic chairs. No quaint Adirondack chairs for Happy Sands renters — these chairs are all about stackability. But any discomfort is made up for with the bright glass of Pinot Blanc in my hand. Martin is in the cabin, lying down in the bedroom. I hope he's not going to be like this all week. I'm no psychologist, but we massage therapists end up knowing a lot. I'm sure he's got depression. Or, as one of my regular clients likes to say, 'the depression.' One of her friends has got 'the cancer.' Another of her friends had a bout with 'the shingles.' I'm always thinking my client has a case of the 'the's.

Alistair is inside on the couch, mad because I unpacked the car. I pretended not to notice while I poured this glass of wine. He should be happy that I unpacked and he doesn't have to help later. He's also probably mad that he doesn't have his phone — going through some initial phone-detox without it. It's an unspoken rule for all the vacationers at Happy Sands: no phones. We left ours at home on the kitchen table. We'll reattach ourselves to them in a week. Perhaps because we do it every year, no one complains — at least, not openly.

I look to the water and see Ruby pirouetting in the sand, the waves lapping over her shoes. Ah, little Ruby. I raise my glass to her, to the beauty of Cornflower Lake, to the white sand beach and Ponderosa pines. But as I drink, I realize Ruby is not aimlessly playing. She is strategically creeping her way towards a group down the beach. It looks like the Roccos — a family she tried to latch on to last summer. It's possible that when Ruby got out of the car and ran, it was not so much to run towards the beach as it was to run away from us, her own family, and to find the Roccos, a better family. A family that probably played I Spy and sang songs and laughed on their drive to Happy Sands. Then I say to myself, Ginny, tomorrow will be smoother, happier. You will swim, massage, find your holiday groove. To help tide you over until then, pour yourself another glass of wine. Okay, I say, I think I will.

DAY 2

The cabin we rent at Happy Sands is the same as everyone else's. Two small bedrooms, a combined kitchen and sitting area, a bathroom with a baby blue toilet with an askew wooden seat, and a baby blue bathtub. Every cabin has a wood-burned sign outside, above the door, that displays a name, like Beehive or Bear Den or Eagle's Loft. Except ours, which doesn't have a sign at all. We are not the tidiest family, and when Martin is 'sleepy,' he closes the blinds, preferring a stale darkness, so I think of our dim messy place as Rat's Nest.

We've only been here one night, and already it is a rat's nest. That's why I stay, as much as I can, on the front deck. It's mid-morning. I'm watching Alistair who is, hurrah, out of the cabin, walking down to the beach. Walking like a crane, his long thin legs still in jeans. How is he not too hot? When he gets close to the water, a little kid — looking maybe like one of the Oliemens who also come every summer, although it's hard to tell for sure because kids change so much over the year, and because I get other people's kids mixed up, which drives my own kids crazy — anyway, a kid runs up and hugs Alistair's leg. Alistair pats the kid on the head, squats to talk to him.

Alistair can be such a good soul. Wait, Ginny, are you the same woman who was complaining about him yesterday? A good night's sleep and not having to work in that stinking room I rent back home at Prairie Physiotherapy can do wonders for the perception. That room has the lingering stench of the patchouli oil used by the hippie therapist who rented the room before me, like twenty years before me. Back then the place must have been almost toxic to anyone with a scent sensitivity. But, other than leftover patchouli in the massage room, Prairie is an okay place to work. The physiotherapists are mostly acceptable. Mostly. What's that joke? The difference between a physiotherapist and God? God doesn't think he's a physiotherapist. It's a relief to work at Happy Sands — on my own without any of them around.

While my perception of Alistair has brightened this morning, my perception of Martin, who is still lying in bed, has not improved. How about 'live your best life'? 'You only go around once'? Okay, okay, cut the syrupy mantras, Ginny. It's a vacation. He wants to sleep in. Other people do. But if he's still asleep at noon, I will be grumpy. I'm already grumpy at him for being depressed. And grumpy at myself for having that uncharitable thought. And grumpy at both of us for not being the kind of couple who get up at the same time, serve each other hot croissants from a wicker basket lined with a checkered cloth, and then hold hands as we stroll towards the beach, confident all along that our bums look firm and cute in our bathing suits, and then, in a moment of spontaneous joy, let go of each other's hands and perform a string of perfect simultaneous cartwheels.

Let it go. Zap. Gone. Martin and I should never do cartwheels on the beach. I'm forty-two years old and it would take me a few glasses of wine, perhaps a bottle, before my mind and muscles would feel loose enough to attempt even one cartwheel. It's the kind of miscalculation I see people in my massage room at Prairie Physiotherapy for — that is, middle-aged people attempting maneuvers they were good at, or mistakenly believe they were good at, decades earlier. But, recognizing the way people my age relive and exaggerate athletic exploits from their youth, I am still going to assert that I was nimble when I was younger. My signature trick in high school was the tinsica — a cartwheel that midway turns into a walkover. These days, the only time I am upside down is when I do a flip-turn at the end of a pool.

Ruby's on an old surfboard, paddling around the swimming area. I suspect she is looking for Moby Trout. Kids at Happy Sands claim to see Moby Trout every summer. I haven't told Ruby that Moby Trout is probably just any random trout they see in the water. I haven't even shared that thought with Alistair — although, at sixteen, I assume he knows. I let Alistair and Ruby find out about all the fake magic in their childhood world the old-fashioned way, i.e. through a shaming comment from someone in their peer group. Some version of, "You don't still believe in that do you?" I've heard of parents who sit their kids down and reveal all the bunk behind the tooth fairy and Santa Claus and the Easter bunny in one crushing swoop. If they're going to be so honest and direct, why not tell them it sucks to be an adult?

I hear Martin moving about the cabin. The sound of shower water would be a good sign. Maybe he's got some energy. Could Martin do a cartwheel? Hard to imagine. He's built like a lamppost — obviously where Alistair gets it from. And he's got lumbar back pain, who doesn't, so he can't do too much, he says. More activity might be good for his spine. Massage would help, but he doesn't like massage, claims it doesn't work for him. It's not so weird. I have colleagues whose partners don't like massage. The one time I gave Martin a massage, he said it hurt like hell. I'd know better now, but at the time I assumed he could tolerate deep tissue work. It was late at night after we'd been drinking beer at a hockey game — way back before Martin became a one-drink party dud. I might have applied more pressure than I planned. Ever since then, if I offer a massage, Martin says he'd rather have a nap.

I look at Alistair, now digging in the sand with the younger boy, and at Ruby, standing on the surfboard and rocking it side to side, and I look across Cornflower Lake and at the cloudless sky, breathe deeply, and think we are lucky.

We get to have this vacation. And how can Martin not be out here? How can this day, this location, not lift him up? I want all the family gears to mesh smoothly, as in previous summers. We played bocce and drank iced tea and read books out loud to each other. We had meaningful conversations, we laughed all the time. Or, wait, that sounds like a curated memory. Maybe I saw that in a movie or read it in a book.

I head into the cabin.

"Hey," Martin says from the bed. "Want some help unpacking the car in a bit?"

"I did it already," I say. "Yesterday."

I wait for some sort of acknowledgement. Don't get it.

"Want to go for a swim with me?" I ask. "The kids are down at the beach."

"Maybe later," Martin says. "I feel like hanging out here. It's a holiday."

I pull my one-piece swimsuit out of the rickety dresser, say, "Oh, well. Maybe you're winding down from work."

This is how we speak. He never says he is depressed. He says he feels like lounging or taking it easy. Or napping. Then I mutter an excuse for him and think nasty thoughts. I never directly say you are tired because you are depressed. We're both in an infinite loop.

Martin works in IT for an oil company. Same job for two decades, just like me. From the way he describes his work, it sounds boring. I've heard that boredom can be depressing. Whenever I ask, "How was your day?" He says, "Still employed." I read somewhere that waiting for an event that never comes, like a layoff package, can be depressing.

Most massage therapists aren't in the kind of employment that involves layoff packages. Although we do sometimes treat the physical results of layoffs: neck pain, sore backs — ironically, maladies that seem like they should be issues that arise when people *are* working, especially in desk jobs, as opposed to not working. I've got a client who has been parachuted out of three jobs — his trapezius muscles feel like car tires.

"Ginny?" Martin says, as I'm straightening the straps on my swimsuit and leaving the room.

I stop in the doorway.

"I hung a paper bag on the deck to keep the wasps away," he says.

"Hey, that's great," I say. Martin believes that a puffed-out paper bag acts as a wasp deterrent by making wasps think there is already a hive there and so they must find another place to reside. I think it looks like garbage. But it's evidence that he left the bedroom. I go over to the bed and lean in to kiss his cheek.

"Whew," he says, accepting the kiss, but turning his head away slightly, "a hint of stale booze there. How much did you drink last night?"

"Two glasses of wine," I say. "It's a holiday."

What is this — the Spanish Inquisition? I drank the whole bottle, because Martin wasn't awake to drink with me.

Down at the beach, Alistair is still helping the little kid build a shape in the sand. Some sort of animal? Yes, I see as I walk closer, it's a fish, with a driftwood fin and a sly beach-pebble eye. Moby Trout, I suppose. And there's Ruby, out of the water now, farther down the beach, with a girl I suspect is the Roccos' daughter. Brie Rocco. Sounds like an expensive appetizer. The Roccos stay in Squirrel Nook. Brie is a smarty-pants like her mother, and a grade or two ahead of Ruby in school, but age doesn't much matter in summer. I see Brie and Ruby stroll up from the beach and walk towards the cabins. I can tell from Ruby's posture, and the way she is swinging her arms, that she is delighted to be in Brie's company.

At Happy Sands, the kids can have summer friends, and all-age friends, and hangout time, and do those lazy activities that, when I was a kid, I always imagined people did 'at the cabin.'

I wade into the water, up to my waist, then turn around, look at the shore once more, before I flop back and start kicking.

After my swim, I wrap my towel around my body, slide into my flip-flops and walk around the resort. Time to drum up some business. I know, it's supposed to be a vacation. But it's far more relaxing here than at Prairie Physio. My own schedule. No pressure. People still need massages. I can help them, and they can help me. A little extra pocket cash never hurts. Every massage is two or three bottles of good Okanagan wine.

Mrs. Edwards is stooped on the deck of her cabin, Beehive, and using a soapy washcloth to clean several plastic pink flamingoes. She brings these flamingoes to Happy Sands in her van, every year. It might even be the reason she has a van. When the flamingoes are scrubbed clean, she will stick them in the sandy grass around Beehive. Mrs. Edwards says she likes the 'holiday atmosphere' they bring to her cabin. I think Mrs. Edwards likes plastic junk. More than she likes people.

Only one person at Happy Sands doesn't call me Ginny. That would be Mrs. Edwards. She's about fifteen years older than me. Maybe not even sixty years old, yet she prefers most people, and all people who work for her in any capacity, to call her 'Mrs. Edwards.' She calls me Ginette. She says nicknames are lazy.

I stop to visit Mrs. Edwards because, by the way she is bent while she washes the flamingoes, I know she is going to hurt her back.

"How's the cleaning going?" I ask.

"Fussy," she says.

I think, fussy — just like you. Those flamingoes don't need to be cleaned. But I say, "That doesn't look like a great position for your back."

"I can feel it already."

"Massage would help. If you'd like, I could come over tonight," I say. Sometimes I have to push my business along.

"Tonight would be fine. Seven p.m."

"Great! See you then!" I say in my best fake-gregarious way. I suspect she doesn't like me that much. But I also know my massages reduce her pain.

On my way back to my cabin, I come across Kathy, who stays in Beaver Lodge, and who is unpacking her hatchback. She's a single mom living in a small village on the nearby desert slopes. She comes to Happy Sands for her annual one week get-away with her now four-year-old twins, Tara and Todd.

"Kathy! Welcome!" I say. "Tough drive?"

"Dreadful," she says. "All twenty minutes."

"And how are the T siblings?"

"Evil."

Tara and Todd run out of the cabin in their bathing suits, holding swim masks and snorkels.

"Ginny!" they scream.

"Tara. Todd," I say, in a way I hope is calming.

Todd throws his plastic face mask in the air, landing it on the roof of the cabin.

"Massage?" I ask Kathy.

"Book me in," Kathy says, as she pulls an armload of towels and a mesh bag of beach toys out of the car.

"Will do. I've got Mrs. Edwards tonight. She's putting her back out washing the flamingoes."

"Same every year," Kathy says. "Can Alistair watch the kids during my massage?"

In previous summers Alistair has had no problem watching Tara and Todd. He taught them how to play toilet tag and gave them airplane rides until they puked. He was their hero. But today, as I walk back to the cabin, I'm thinking that Alistair is not going to be pleased that I've committed him to an hour of babysitting. Too bad, I decide. An hour won't kill him. Kathy works twice as hard as anyone I know, especially Alistair, and she deserves to have her massage.

I open the door to my cabin. Inside it's dark, even though the sun is blazing outside. The thick brocade curtains are drawn over all the windows. Every year, I leave a comment on our renter form about those curtains. Why are they here? Did they come from the set of an Elizabethan drama? When my eyes adjust, I take in that Alistair has returned from the beach and is in the main room, and Martin is still lying on the bed in the bedroom.

Alistair has folded himself onto the short couch. His kneecaps protrude like a couple of hardboiled eggs. It is the world's most uncomfortable couch, like a thinly upholstered park bench, and Alistair's angular body makes it look even more punishing. If Alistair wants to lie down, why doesn't he lie on the chaise lounge at the beach? Why doesn't Martin lie on a chaise lounge at the beach? News alert: we're on a beach vacation!

I pull apart the curtains. "Let the sunshine in," I sing.

"Noooo," Alistair whines. Maybe because of the light or maybe because of my singing.

"Hi, Al," I say in my happy-mommy tone. What I want to say is, listen up, when I was kid I would've given anything for a week holiday at a lake, and I would have spent every possible second outside.

Alistair covers his eyes with his hands. Just like he would have if I'd made a geriatric, and probably untrue, comment that started with 'When I was I kid . . .'

I walk into the bedroom where Martin is 'sleeping.'

"Marty?" I ask. "Are you awake?"

"Okay," he says.

"Okay?"

"Okay. I'll be up in a minute. I know that's what you're after."

"Thanks," I say, and give him a kiss. And then regret it. Why should I give him thanks and a kiss? Shouldn't he be up anyway? Is that really what I am after? Is that all I am after?

Martin does not get up in a minute. At dinner time, he is still in bed. What does he do in there? Lying down that long is hard on a person's spine. And joints. If this napping keeps up, he's going to have to worry about bedsores.

I put the Waifs' "Sink or Swim" on the CD player, toss some pork chops in the marinade, and turn on the barbecue. I open a beer and call out, "Happy hour," with as much cheerful passive-aggression as I can muster.

"I'll have a beer," Alistair says from the couch.

"Sure," I say, "when you're old enough."

As I light the barbecue, Ruby runs up to the deck. I haven't seen her for hours. I should have been worrying. In the city, I would have been worrying. But that's the beauty of Happy Sands. Everyone looks out for everyone. Or maybe that's the way it was in a novel I read once. You know, the kind of story where all the kids are running around in a pack and secretly solving a mystery and never seem to require a meal or a parent . . . except at the climax of the story, when things get dangerous, and then the parents show up and save the day even though they were too dumb to solve the mystery.

"Can I eat dinner at the Roccos'?" she asks.

"Were you invited?"

"Mom," Ruby says, exasperated with me.

"All right." I meant invited by an adult. Not just by Brie. But what do I care if Brie's mother is unprepared for a dinner guest? Who am I kidding? Brie's mother is the type who is prepared for everything. And no doubt she's cooking up something better than pork chops.

I watch Ruby skip across the sandy common area to Brie's cabin, and wish I had said that she needed to have dinner with us, her own family. But there was no reason to say that. Just a whim of mine.

I go inside and get a beer from the fridge for myself, and another that I hand to Alistair.

"You can have a beer if you come out on the deck and drink it with me."

And he does. And it is not entirely enjoyable, at least from my point of view, because I have bribed him with alcohol to be with me. But Alistair is pleasant.

"Was that an Oliemen kid you were building sand stuff with?" I ask.

"Yeah. Bart."

"He's grown. I think of Bart as a baby."

"I'm avoiding him. He talks too much."

Is that a signal to me? Do I talk too much? Am I asking too many questions? Or just an observation that Bart does talk too much? I decide to not pursue my questions with another question.

Alistair finishes his beer in boat-race time. Clearly, it's not his first. I should say something to him about alcohol. Something about moderation. How he has to learn to keep it between the posts. How the drunkest person at the party never has the most fun. How alcohol is a drug. The whole spiel. Then I think I will save the advice for when he asks for another beer. Why ruin this moment with a lecture?

The wind kicks up and blows beach sand in our direction.

"Let's eat dinner inside," Alistair says.

"Sure," I say, "Go on in. I'll do the barbecuing."

I don't know why I say that. Because I am so pathetically grateful to have his company for fifteen minutes? But, okay, it's the first full day of holidays, everyone should do what makes them happy. Martin in bed, Alistair watching cartoons, Ruby with another family. And me barbecuing in a sandstorm. Oh, wait, that doesn't make me happy. Another beer will make me happy.

While I barbecue, I think about that song, *Let the sun shine in / Meet it with a grin.* And I remember that the next line is, *Smilers never lose, and frowners never win.*

If only.

After dinner I pull my massage table out of the car. I store it in the car so it doesn't take up space in the cabin, and so there's no chance it will get spilled on or used as a drying rack for wet bathing suits and towels. The table is still in its canvas carrying case. I put one strap over my head and across my body, like a monstrous messenger bag. There's a handle on the side of the case that I lift with, to soften the weight on my shoulder. The final step is to loop my tote — a woven sack containing a set of sheets, my notebook and my oils and lotions — over my other shoulder. Thus burdened, I walk as normally as possible to Mrs. Edward's cabin, Beehive. It's still daylight when I arrive. The flock of flamingoes doesn't look too disturbing — yet. Once night falls, it is hard to see their metal legs or the black tip of their beaks, making them appear as a floating mash-up of body parts: the torso half of a giant heart, the neck a stretched section of colon. Mrs. Edward's daughter, Esther, who's the same age as Alistair, answers the door after I knock. Esther and Mrs. Edwards usually eat inside, at a properly set table. All the cabins have barbecues out front, but Mrs. Edwards prefers the oven. Chicken in mushroom soup, lasagna, that sort of thing. She says barbecues are dirty.

Mrs. Edwards is a widow. Word on the beach is that she nagged her husband to death. Beach gossip is the cruellest gossip. I massaged Mr. Edwards once, several years ago, and the whole time I worried that my portable table was going to collapse. Facedown, he hung right over the sides. Forget about rolling him over on the table. I had to ask him to get off the table, stand up, and then lie back on the table, faceup. He was very gracious about it all. A nice guy. But, with his size and the constricted way he was breathing and the weight limit of my portable table, I worried he might die during treatment. It was the only time I ever had that worry. It's difficult, though not impossible, to kill someone with a massage.

Mrs. Edwards is uptight about everything. But, through some strange twist of reasoning, she likes the flamingoes and seems okay with Esther's goth uniform: studded arm bands, collars, an utterly black wardrobe, and Marilyn Manson makeup. Esther, at least in the summer, usually looks more overheated than ghoulish.

I start to haul my massage table inside.

"I could carry that table," Esther says. "I've been working out."

"Good on you," I say. I think, maybe you can come over to Rat's Nest and show my guys how to work out.

Although it's late in the day, the temperature is at least 25°C outside, and warmer inside Beehive, Esther wears a thick long-sleeved black shirt. She's cut, or stabbed, a hole in the material at each wrist so that she can stick her thumb through. She also wears a baggy pair of black jeans with a thick silver chain that starts at one front pocket, loops down to her knee, and then rises up to the back pocket and appears to serve no purpose whatsoever.

"Where do you work out?" I ask.

"At a gym. Not a stretchy pants mom-yoga place. Free weights. Open twenty-four hours."

Mrs. Edwards comes into the room in a Hugh Hefner-type robe that she wears before and after massages. When she wears that red robe with the black lapels — which she has worn for at least ten summers — she even looks a bit like the Hef.

The only place my open table fits in Beehive, or any cabin at Happy Sands, is in the main room or on the front deck. Mrs. Edwards likes the main room. I take the table out of the carrying case, spread the sides apart, stand it up, then add the fitted sheet, flat sheet, and flannel cover on the face cradle. To respect Mrs. Edwards' privacy and maintain a professional boundary, I stand in the bathroom when it's time for her to disrobe and climb between the sheets on the massage table. It's all a bit nonsensical. I'm going to see most of her nude body anyway, albeit in sections, because I drape the parts I'm not working on. Honestly, I couldn't care less how Mrs. Edwards looks in the raw.

While I wait, I wash my hands in warm water in the bathroom sink so that they are clean and won't be cold when I touch her skin. I check in the mirror for crow's feet in the corners of my eyes. Still there. I practise standing with good posture, turn sideways, shoulders back, gut in.

"Ginette, I'm ready," Mrs. Edwards calls impatiently from the main room.

Whoopee, I think. But then I remind myself that I can help Mrs. Edwards. And I have a week here, so I'll need six bottles of Pinot.

Mrs. Edwards is the type who will soon have trouble opening jars. Trim but gooey. She has a flat bum. No muscle there at all. I don't know what she thinks she's hiding, or protecting, by keeping her underwear on. People are funny that way. I mean, underwear can reveal more about a person than a bare bum. Mrs. Edwards, for instance, sports a standard high-rise pair. Yet I am surprised at the racy black and white checked fabric. Absolutely NASCAR. I can't wait to tell Martin. Naw, he's currently not in the mood to find that entertaining. Besides, it's not ethical to talk about a client's underwear to other people. Okay, I do. But only to Martin.

I pour a few drops of massage oil in my palm, warm it by rubbing my hands together. Then it's time to work. I start on the left side of Mrs. Edwards' neck. She has the body woes that typically impede her female age group. Sore lower back caused mainly by weak core muscles and tight scalene muscles resulting in a slouched posture. She never exercises. But unlike most other women I treat, she is not the kind who carries stress in her body. She says whatever she feels like. Instead, she's one of those who export stress to others. It's highly possible I will leave here needing a massage. I haven't had a massage in years. Who would meet my standards?

"Have you seen the new renter?" Mrs. Edwards asks, once I start working on her.

"Staying at Happy Sands?"

"Young guy. He looks like he exercises all day. Just your type. He's staying in Fish Bowl."

"Aren't the Wilsons in Fish Bowl? They come every summer."

"Apparently not. Stop that. Not so deep," Mrs. Edwards orders.

"Sorry," I say. "I'll lighten up."

I wasn't working that deep. I *lightly* continue my way down the sides of Mrs. Edward's spine. Her racetrack checkers are in the way, preventing me from doing effective work on her lower back and hip. I try my best. I fold her underwear down a bit; the elastic flips them back up with a snap. I work my way back up, focus on her neck again, finish with a scalp massage, which I haven't tried on her before but which, judging from her relaxed breathing, is a good strategy.

"Do you want a massage, too?" I ask Esther before I go to stand in the bathroom so Mrs. Edwards can get off the table and put her weird robe back on.

"No, she does not," Mrs. Edwards says. "This one's costing enough."

"I don't like people touching me," Esther says.

That seems like solid fodder for a psychotherapist, not a massage therapist. Time to leave Beehive. Hey, Ginny, I think to myself as I tip my table onto its side, tuck in the legs, and fold it in half, there's a glass of wine waiting for you at Rat's Nest. Hey, thanks, Ginny, I think in reply, I'm looking forward to it. I've earned it.

Mrs. Edwards hands me a cheque. She is the only client who still uses cheques, even though at Prairie Physio I have several clients who are older than her. I've always told everyone at Happy Sands that my services here are cash only. But it's not worth it to say no thanks to Mrs. Edwards' cheque. I'll cash it after our vacation.

In my rush to get out of Beehive, I don't put my table back in the travel case. The table has a side handle that I can use to lug it around for the rest of the week. I tuck the empty case under one arm and the table under the other arm, and hang my tote bag with the sheets and oils around my neck. I carry the whole kit and kaboodle to the car, where it will sit until the next massage.

When I return to our cabin, Alistair and Martin are sitting in the dark in front of the television. They have redrawn the curtains. Martin, in grey sweats and a floral shirt, seems to be asleep. Alistair, in nothing but boxers, seems to be watching a show about oceans. He eats a pork chop. I don't tell him to get a plate. Or a shirt. But I'd like to. And I'd like to say to them both, manners alert, how about a hello when I walk in the cabin, or, reaching for the moon here, how about asking about how my massage went with Mrs. Edwards?

"A guy came by asking about massage," Alistair says.

"What guy?"

"Dunno. Never seen him before."

"What did he look like?" I say. I refrain from saying that 'dunno' is not a real word.

"Happy."

"That's it?"

"Yep. One of those wide-smile guys." Alistair takes another bite of the pork chop. "And he's ripped. He's been to the gym."

While I'm pouring my glass of wine and imagining what the jacked happy guy thought of these two louts sitting in the dark, Ruby enters the cabin.

She flicks on the room lights, asks, "Can I go for a night swim with the Roccos?"

"Sure," I say. "Want me to come?"

"That's okay," Ruby says.

She sprints out of the cabin, not wasting any time on us family-folk. The light is still on after she leaves. Everything is a bit brighter in the cabin, at least on the surface. I'm a teensy bit hurt that Ruby didn't want me to come with her, but I get it — who wants their mom along on a night swim with another family? I love that she is out doing a Happy Sands activity, and I love that she has turned on the light. If anyone moves to turn that light off, I will pounce on them like a rabid wolverine.

Later that night, before I go to bed, I check on Ruby. She's lying on her bed reading a book, her hair still wet from swimming with the Roccos. I kiss the top of her head. She keeps reading but waggles her fingers in my face — acknowledging the kiss, and, at the same time, waving me away. I'll take what I can get. Back in the kitchen, Alistair is up and making toast. I say my goodnight, stand on my toes and kiss him on the cheek. He pats me on the shoulder. I realize I'm like a dog going through a house looking for affection. In the bedroom, I get into my pajamas — an ancient shorts-and-top baby doll set that I bring to Happy Sands every year because nothing works better to keep me cool during the warm Okanagan nights. I spoon in behind Martin, pressing into his back, listen to the waves outside lapping the beach, the slight breeze in the trees behind the cabins, Martin's deep, slow breathing. I give him a hug, and he pats my arm, and then inches away from me.

I roll toward the wall and wonder about the new guy at Happy Sands. How ripped is he? How happy?

DAY 3

The seven cabins at Happy Sands are arranged in a horseshoe around the waterfront so everyone has a view of the firepit, the beach, and Cornflower Lake. Our cabin is in the middle, at the top of the horseshoe. Or the bottom of the horseshoe — depending on your perspective. A cowboy client once told me that horseshoes should be hung with the heels, or open sides, up, otherwise your luck will run out. That guy had loose elbow ligaments from bull riding. They were like overstretched elastic bands — never going to return to form.

The cabins rented by the Oliemens and Roccos are at the heels of the horseshoe. Oliemens are in Bear Den; Roccos are in Squirrel Nook. Both families usually arrive a day ahead of us. They own motorboats with assorted boards and skis and inflatable structures to be towed behind their boats. They are sporty, outdoorsy families of the type that I always wished I grew up in. So long as there is daylight and the water is relatively calm, they are boating. Some days they don't even come in for lunch. They bring a cooler of drinks and food and hook their boats together for lunch. The women are gym-fit and spend their winters practising whatever spawn-of-Jane-Fonda aerobics class is in fashion. Zumba, bikini boot camp, CrossFit, Tabata, any of the new riffs on yoga. I'm guessing here, based on what most of my female clients show up injured from these days. In a just and fair world, the trendy exercise classes and the powerboat toys would result in minor soft tissue injuries and more business for me at Happy Sands. And yet, I have never massaged a Rocco or an Oliemen. Not one pulled hamstring from skiing or one torqued rotator cuff from wakeboarding. Maybe they go elsewhere, or maybe they never feel the need. Either way, I'm left with the tiring unpaid job of having to pretend that it doesn't bother me.

The Rocco and Oliemen kids are a blonde passel of pre-teens. All younger than Alistair, mostly older than Ruby. The Oliemens are from the old-money part of Calgary, and while the kids are quiet, the wife, Darla, livens up the place by throwing a temper tantrum now and then. Last summer, I witnessed, from this very deck, Darla slamming the barbecue cover up and down while yelling that she was done cooking for her family. Right now, as I drink my first coffee of the morning, I look toward Bear Den and watch Darla escalating once again to that barbecue-slamming emotional state. She marches — and by 'marches' I mean the angry-mom march that is common throughout the world, I've done it myself many times — out of their cabin and down to the dock and then back to the cabin. Her husband, Doug, is getting their boat ready to go for the day. The water is calm. 'Butter,' they call it. Perfect for powerboating activities. The Oliemen children, towels flopped across their groggy shoulders, are stumbling across the beach toward the boat. My kids, Ruby and Alistair, won't be awake for hours. I probably should feel smug that I let my kids sleep in, but I don't. I want them to get their carcasses out of bed and do something. But what? Jog? Do a set of burpees and jumping jacks? If I let Martin sleep, then I have to let the kids sleep.

Oh, here I go. I do realize it's only a small step from any direction or topic for me to blame everything on Martin.

"Doug! Jackass!" Darla shouts from the door of Bear Den to the dock, where Doug is loading the boat with wakeboards and skis. "Where's the cooler?"

Doug waves at her, gives her a thumbs up — apparently trying to suggest that he doesn't hear her, but that all is good. Darla ramps up the volume and screams, "Do I have to do everything myself? Is no one in this family capable of anything?"

The cabin door closes. Hard. Then it opens and Darla steps out long enough to yell, "I'm not your servant, people."

I admire Darla's ability to yell. To not care what other people might think or whose feelings might by crushed. To convey her thoughts to another person so clearly and immediately and sometimes cruelly. And I am slightly intimidated. What if she were to yell at me like that? Maybe I'm lucky that she never asks me for a massage.

Then the Rocco kids, the other boat family, file out of their cabin like sleepwalkers. Brie is there, in line with the rest. They get in their boat. Curl up in the bow seats on their towels. When the adult Roccos come down to the dock and get in their boat, they wave at Doug in his boat. Doug points at his cabin, shrugs.

Eventually Darla comes out of the cabin dragging a big cooler by one handle. Clearly in a fury. She pulls it off the deck, bump bump bump, down the stairs and drags it across the sand to the boat dock. No one helps. Probably scared to. I'm certainly not going down there.

The Roccos are from Canmore. They've been friends with the Oliemens for years, and, en route to Happy Sands, usually meet on the TransCanada highway so as to create a two-SUV, two-boat, sporty-people convoy. Shelley Rocco is a foodie. She's been to cooking classes all over Europe, and she'll tell you all about them if you aren't careful to avoid all possible segues to the topic. Shelley keeps a look on her face that I assume she thinks makes her look like a talented television chef who must deal with kitchen imbeciles all day, but, in fact, makes her look like she is holding in a fart. I know the look, I've seen my clients holding in farts, especially if I am doing an abdominal massage. And I spend a lot of time holding in farts myself, because letting one rip isn't professional. Occasionally a toot escapes, and I convince myself that the generic 1970s pop music, which I always have playing in the massage room in Prairie Physiotherapy, has covered it up.

The boating men, Doug Oliemen and Ricky Rocco, met in high school. Now in their forties, they haven't grown up much. At least, not since I've known them. Their vacations are measured by a catalogue of which kid did what first: swim to the raft, wake surf, slalom ski. A conversation of any length with either of them usually strays from the children's accomplishments to anecdotes about Doug and Ricky's own athletic exploits, which, despite many embellishments, are boring. Who cares about the cross-country cycle trip they took twenty years ago, or the depth of their annual winter scuba dives off Belize?

Obviously, I've never been tight with the Oliemens or Roccos. It might be because they are usually gone all day, out on the water. Martin says I have a chip on my shoulder about the Oliemens and Roccos because they never hire me. I'd like to think I am bigger than that.

After the Rocco and Oliemen boats have zipped a short way from the dock and stopped, and after one kid has plopped out of each boat, and after the boats have zoomed off again, each pulling the kid on a ski, I pour myself another coffee and go for a quiet stroll along the beach. Barefoot, relaxed, I feel like someone out of a holiday advertisement. Then I reach the sand version of Moby Trout that Alistair and the little kid made yesterday. Someone has crafted a giant sand penis on Moby's fish body. Who would do such a thing? Maybe I'll find it funny later in the day. Maybe I can lure Martin down to the beach with the promise of some sand porn.

I circle back to the car and haul out my massage table and tote bag. Last night Dot and Ruthanne, the elderly couple in Eagle's Loft, left a note for me to come this morning. Seniors can be slow getting their clothes on and off, and slow getting on and off the table, and thus turn an hour appointment into an hour-and-a-half appointment. But not Dot and

Ruthanne. Even a few of my non-senior clients take forever to get changed. At Prairie Physio, I sometimes end up standing outside the massage room door repeatedly asking ready? Ready? And getting the answer 'not yet' or 'just a sec,' and it makes me wonder what sort of contraptions these people are wearing. Novelty buttons on their underwear? Ornamental bras? But when I do go into the room and look on the chair where their clothes are piled, I see only regular garments. Which isn't to say they haven't hidden something wacky at the bottom of the pile. People rarely put their underclothing at the top of the pile, where I can see it, even though that's the item that they took off last.

Dot and Ruthanne, each holding a ceramic mug, sit in plastic chairs on their deck. The same chairs that we have on our deck, on every deck, at Happy Sands. Beside them on the deck, two inflated air mattresses lean against the railing. When Dot sees me, she gives me a cheery wave, and goes inside to get ready for her massage.

"Morning, Ginny," Ruthanne says from her seat. She raises her mug to me. "Coffee?"

"No, thanks," I say. "I've had enough coffee this morning."

I'm always careful with coffee, and other diuretics, on massage days. It's hard to deliver an effective massage when you are focusing on your own bladder. "Been out on the mattresses yet?"

"We had a good float last night. We've been going later, when the boats aren't out, and it's quieter."

"My family always talks about buying air mattresses," I say. In fact, it's usually just me talking about buying an air mattress for the holiday, and nobody in the family responds. I don't push it because I don't think I have the gene for relaxation, for drifting about on a floatie.

"Oh, don't bother," Ruthanne says. "Borrow ours anytime."

"Looks like Dot's up first today," I say, pointing to Dot's empty chair.

"We played rock paper scissors. She won. Go on in and get set up."

Inside, the main room has already been prepared for me, the furniture pushed to the sides to make space for the massage table. I open the table, attach the head piece. I start unfolding the sheets I've brought. I hear the sound of the toilet flushing, and Dot comes out of the bathroom. She's little, dot-ish, with a spikey gray haircut, and wears a T-shirt and Lycra shorts. I assume that Dot has always been small, it's not just old-age shrinkage, by the way she moves around the room, scrambling on a chair to reach the top of the curtains so she can partially close them.

"All ready, here," I say.

Dot starts taking off her T-shirt with no bra underneath, while telling me through the uplifting fabric that she's been experiencing some numbness in her right foot.

"I better run to the bathroom," I say. I'll never get used to seeing my nude clients when they are upright. It's a whole different perspective, and I feel like I am breaking some massage therapist code of ethics by looking at Dot.

"No rush," Dot says as she snaps off her shirt and starts to pull down her shorts.

When I come back from the bathroom, where I have flushed the toilet so that Dot thinks I really had to go, Dot has climbed onto the table and between the sheets. I pull the top sheet up to cover all of her back and with my hands on the sheet, I gently rock her muscles to warm them up. She is eighty. I don't want to bruise her or tear her papery skin.

"Deeper," Dot says. "I'm not paying you for a fluff and buff."

Deeper? I could break one of her bones if I apply too much pressure. But I lower the top sheet. I get some unscented oil from my tote bag, warm a squirt of it with friction between my hands, and then press my hands, flat, under her scapula. She's got some old divots on her upper back from skin cancer removal. I don't see any wonky moles or evidence of new cancer there.

"For Pete's sake, Ginny," Dot says. "Get therapeutic on me."

"Do as she says," Ruthanne advises as she comes in from the deck. She sits at the kitchen table, flips through a magazine, says, "Dot's a real bag if she doesn't get her own way."

"Isn't that the pot calling the kettle black," Dot says through the headpiece of my massage table. I can feel her body shake, because she is laughing. Dot laughs a lot. Where do I sign up for a roommate like that? Where do I sign up to be like that?

I work over Dot's upper torso, and down her legs, particularly her right leg, where she has some sciatica. When the hour is almost over, Ruthanne stands up beside the kitchen table. She pulls off her shirt, a purple bra-top, and drapes it on the back of the chair. I try to focus on Dot's treatment, but it's hard with big nude Ruthanne there.

"Ruthanne," I say, "no rush. I need to change the sheets. And then I'll give you some privacy to get changed."

"I'm eighty-two years old. What do I care if you see me get undressed? And unless Dot messed the bed, I don't care if we use the same sheets."

"I haven't lost control over my bowels yet," Dot says, chuckling, as she slides off the table and strolls over to the sink for a glass of water.

Ruthanne pulls off her pants and starts to climb onto the bed. She's tall, with broad shoulders and a belly. And not nimble enough to get on the table easily. I hustle around, try to adjust the sheets under her, try to preempt any falls, and try to ignore the wide-open visual of her rear end as she struggles to get on the table. I love all the different styles and ages of bodies I get to see in my job, but, as with Ruthanne's bum in this situation, there can be a point of too much information. On one of her saggy glutes she's got a tattoo of a cat smoking a cigarette. Not the first time I've seen this tattoo of Ruthanne's, and, in fact, not the only smoking cat tattoo I've seen on a client. But I never ask about tattoos. That would be unprofessional.

"How's your family?" Ruthanne asks, once I've draped her bum and legs with the top sheet and started in earnest on her shoulder, which has a history of being troublesome. "I've seen the kids at the beach, but not Martin."

"Alistair is going into Grade 11 in the fall. Ruby into Grade 3," I say.

"And Martin?" she asks.

"He's sleeping in." I've known Ruthanne for several summers, and I think she will understand. Surely she will know by my tone that Martin is depressed.

"Well, nothing wrong with sleeping," she says. "Some people love their sleep."

I find the knot in Ruthanne's shoulder, dig in. Ruthanne grunts. I lighten the pressure a bit. It's not my job to burden clients with my problems, so I don't go into detail about how much Martin is horizontal. Nothing is worse than a massage therapist who talks too much. I've had clients tell me that's why they left their previous therapist.

"Everyone happy?" Ruthanne asks.

"You bet," I say.

It takes concentration and technique to loosen the adhesions in Ruthanne's back. But her body is responsive to treatment. I always feel like I have helped Ruthanne. It's the best part of being a massage therapist — knowing that I've made someone feel better in their body. It's hard to be happy if your body is hurting. It's hard enough to be happy under perfect conditions.

"Have you seen the new guy?" Ruthanne asks when the session is almost over.

I'm finishing with a foot massage, something both Dot and Ruthanne like. "Not yet," I say. "Mrs. Edwards told me about him. And Alistair told me he dropped by the cabin."

"We saw him through the window of Fish Bowl," Dot pipes in. She has pulled her clothes back on and is sitting at the kitchen table. "He's good looking. An improvement over the Wilson family. None of them had much of a chin."

"Addendum," Ruthanne says. "He's good looking if you like the traditional action-hero beefcake type."

"I do!" says Dot. "That's why I'm with you."

Ruthanne, still on the bed, blows Dot a kiss.

As I walk back to the cabin, I see Ruby down at Squirrel Nook, knocking on the Roccos' door. Then she peers in the window. Knocks again. I set my tote and massage table down and walk over to her.

"Morning, Ruby. The Roccos went out in the boat."

"Already?" she asks.

"Already," I say.

Ruby crosses her arms, says, "Brie was supposed to play with me today."

"There will be time later. And there are other kids around today. And Alistair."

"Oh, Alistair. He's like Dad. He won't be up until noon."

"You could come for a swim with me," I say.

Ruby makes a face. What could be more boring than swimming with her mother? Then her face brightens. "Canoe?" she suggests.

"You're on," I say. And my heart sings. I get to spend the rest of the morning in a canoe with my daughter. This is what family vacations are all about.

Just then a young man comes down the steps of Fish Bowl and walks across the resort towards us. Long shorts, showing a bit of boxer elastic at the waist, a washed-out muscle shirt — all in all a fair bit of coverage for the beach scene, but it's obvious he's spent time looking in the full length mirror at the gym and feeling darn pleased with his reflection. He's a fittie. Not a sinewy long-distance runner with hamstrings like high-voltage cable, and not a strong-man with pecs the size of chickens — I've had to massage a few of those guys before, and working on them is like trying to loosen up a rock. This guy's just right.

"You must be the massage therapist," he says, when he gets closer. He extends a hand. "Dwayne Champion." There's no indication that he is joking.

"Ginny," I say, shaking his hand, and getting a strong waft of mint.

"Strong grip," he says with a smile.

"Goes with the profession," I say.

And then I giggle. At the same time, I think, oh, no, Ginny, stop. You are too old and cranky to giggle.

Ruby looks at me with her 'what's-with-you' expression. She turns to Dwayne and says, "Me and my mom are going canoeing."

"That's great," Dwayne says. "If your mom has time after, maybe I can book a massage with her."

"Yeah, maybe," Ruby says. "She's usually pretty busy."

"Of course," I say. "We'll set something up. I'll drop by your cabin." I put my arm around Ruby's shoulders, start to steer her towards the beach.

"Cash only," she says to Dwayne.

Is that how Ruby has heard me say 'cash only' to people here? With that sneer? I doubt it.

"Got it," Dwayne says.

I smile at Dwayne — one of those kids-will-be-kids smiles — and Ruby and I continue to the beach.

"Why do you have to work on vacation?" Ruby asks.

"Dwayne's probably sore from working out," I say. "I can help."

"He stinks," Ruby says.

"It's just mint," I say. "I've smelled worse."

Ruby covers her ears to end the conversation. I wasn't going to tell her what smelled worse. Last year Ruby would have found it funny. This year she thinks every story reflects poorly on her, even if it does not involve her. For the record, it might have been the client who came into Prairie Physio with dog poop on her shoe one time. She didn't realize the smell was coming from her shoes until she was getting dressed after the treatment. She never came back for another treatment.

Ruby and I paddle along the shore, away from Happy Sands, towards a reed-filled bay. The water is smooth, the canoe is Canadiana red, and the image an Okanagan postcard. And, okay, okay, every time a motorboat goes by, Ruby studies it to see if it is the Roccos', and if it might be going into the Happy Sands dock. No amount of paddling and holiday scenery can distract me from the fact that I am Ruby's plan B.

Once we get to the reeds, Ruby hangs over the bow of the canoe, looking for fish and blood suckers. I don't love the brush of the reeds against my forearm when I paddle. And while I am not squeamish, I also don't love the flies and tiny moths that drop from the reed tops into our boat.

"Do you think Moby Trout would be swimming here?" Ruby asks.

"Sure," I say. "He's everywhere." Then I regret saying that. Not because I am lying, but because it makes Moby Trout sound like a beachy Big Brother. Like the fish is running surveillance on us.

"Well, that's impossible," she says. "He's a fish. He can't be everywhere at the same time."

More flies drop into the canoe from the reeds. When I can reach them, I use the makeshift bailer, an old plastic bleach bottle, to scoop them out into the water. I could one-up Ruby and say Moby Trout is nowhere. Moby Trout is a myth. But why crush the moment? Why crush Ruby?

Eventually, Ruby sits up, and we agree to paddle back to Happy Sands. We are both itchy, maybe from the flies, maybe from the heat of the day. As we paddle back to the beach, I look up to the cabins and see a large square object, like a giant suitcase, near Fish Bowl. Tara and Todd are jumping on it. Those brats. It's my massage table. Still sitting where I left it when I went to talk to Ruby. And then Dwayne showed up. I've never forgotten my table anywhere before.

Ruby and I pull the canoe onto the beach, turn it over. We place our paddles under it, ready for the next happy users.

I do an angry-mom march towards the massage table. Tara and Todd wave at me as I approach. They are eating popsicles. When I get closer, I can see purple popsicle syrup dripping into the crease of the folded table. I have this one tool of my trade and they are wrecking it.

"Hey, you guys," I say quietly, even though I feel like yelling.

They keep jumping so I say a little louder, "Hey, that's expensive. It's not a trampoline." I am thinking, get off that table or I'll ram those popsicles down your throats. Tara and Todd seem to read my mind because, looking suddenly frightened, they leap off the table and sprint to their cabin.

I crouch beside the table, grab the side handle, and hoist it as I stand. Ruby comes up behind me, picks up my tote. I start walking, but have to stop almost immediately because something is stuck on my foot. I set everything down. Look at my foot, remove the popsicle stick, wipe my foot on the sand to try and remove the purple sugar-glue.

"Do we have any popsicles in our fridge?" Ruby asks.

"No. Tell your dad to get off his butt and get some," I say.

"Okay," she says.

I feel bad about my grumpiness. I should talk to Ruby about the value of my massage equipment. She probably knows already. I should take back what I said about Martin. I do want him off his ass, but I don't want him to buy popsicles. He could buy the kids some fruit. Or buy me a bottle of wine.

"Is it lunch time?" she asks.

"Yep."

"Maybe Brie will come in off the water for lunch."

Oh, good grief. She can't let it go. I can't think of a non-nasty response, so I say instead, "I hope your dad and Alistair are awake."

"Why?" Ruby asks.

Irritating but fair question. What do I care if they sleep the holiday away? Is it hurting me? No. But I think Martin is setting a bad example by lying around the whole time. Not that Martin can help it. And not that you can catch depression from someone else. Well, maybe you can. I'm no doctor. And, deep down, I know what is really bugging me is that it's hard to have family time when part of the family is asleep.

"I don't know," I say to Ruby. And that seems to be a sufficient answer for her. Then, she asks if she and Brie can go canoeing later.

"Sure," I say.

I give my massage table a pat. Ginny's old pal. It's going to be just you and me.

In the afternoon, I'm walking along the road, returning from a fruit stand nearby. The fruit stand runs on the honour system — take your fruit, then leave the money in a wooden box attached to the stand. The prices are painted on the stand — they haven't changed in years. One summer I saw a woman take a carton of cherries and not pay. I thought of pointing out to her that the cherries were not free, but then I thought of reasons why maybe she didn't pay. Forgot her money? Coming back later? And in the end, I never said anything. But I know she was stealing those cherries.

In one hand I'm carrying a bag full of cucumbers; in the other I have a bag of canary melons. My arms feel like they are stretching to the ground. The narrow straps around my hands are cutting off the circulation to my fingers. I would reprimand any client who carried two heavy bags like this.

I hear footsteps behind me. A jogger. A fast jogger. Joggers like to be called runners, I remind myself. I've offended a few clients by making that mistake.

Dwayne pulls up alongside me. "Want some help?" he says, slowing to a walk. He's wearing a running singlet and loose running shorts and some runners that look like they were made in a fluorescent factory.

"Sure," I say. I hand him the cucumbers. I think about making a joke about not touching my melons and then thank all the gods in the universe that I did not make that comment. Instead I ask, "Are you related to the Wilsons?"

"The Wilsons?"

"The people who usually stay in Fish Bowl this week."

"I don't know any Wilsons. Just happened on it. Friend of a friend of friend sort of connection."

We walk along in silence. He in his light fast runners, me in my clunky practical sandals. I don't know why I bought so many melons. My hands are sweating. He smells more minty than sweaty. Seriously minty. I wonder if he has a wife or partner who should be telling him that he stinks. Not that I would tell Martin if he stank like that. But I might hide the aftershave or liniment or body wash or whatever was making my eyes water.

"You have family here besides Ruby?" he asks.

"My husband and son," I say. "You?"

"I'm on my own," he says.

I'm not sure if he means he's a full-time bachelor or if he just means he doesn't have family staying with him this week.

I don't want to pry. Well, I do. But I don't want to look like I am overly interested in him.

At the entrance to Happy Sands, I see Darla Oliemen and Shelley Rocco walking towards us. Dwayne smiles and says hello to them. I nod. Give a fake smile. They give fake smiles back. I guess they were allowed off the ski boats this afternoon. Or maybe the water is too choppy for water sports. They wear fashion flip-flops and short shorts and are probably headed to the same fruit stand I went to . . . probably to buy more fashionable fruit than canary melons.

"So, Ginny," Dwayne says. "I'm training for the MetaMan triathlon."

"I heard."

"And my hip is flaring up."

"I can help. Give me a few minutes to take my stuff home, and I'll come over to your place." I hold out my hand for the cucumbers.

"I'll carry them in," he says.

"No worries," I say, grabbing the cucumbers. "I think my husband might be having a nap, and I don't want to wake him." I *know* my husband is having a nap.

I enter our dark Rat's Nest, set my bags on the kitchen counter. As usual, I leave the cabin door ajar, pull apart the curtains and crank the windows wide. I don't know if fresh air helps Martin, but it sure helps me. Once the room is lit, I see Alistair on the couch. He opens his eyes a slit.

"Hello Alley-bean," I say.

"Hi, Mom," he says.

"Hi, Ginny," Martin says from the bedroom.

"I've brought some Okanagan produce to brighten your day," I say. "Who wants some cucumber or melon?"

"Thanks, not hungry right now," Martin says.

"Did you get any pop?" Alistair asks.

"I was only at the fruit stand," I say. "They're not growing pop this season."

"It was a joke," Alistair says.

I decide to chop a few of the cucumbers immediately. Put the slices into a ziplock bag. A gift for Dwayne.

I'm crossing the space between the cabins, sliced cucumbers and tote in one hand, massage table handle in the other hand with the table itself under my arm, when I notice Dwayne hop down the stairs of his deck. He meets me halfway and gently takes the table from me.

"Hey, this is heavy," he says.

"I'm used to it," I say. But nice to have someone notice.

"Where should I put it?" Dwayne asks.

"We can set it up in your living room or on your deck. Some people don't like the deck because it's not very private. But seeing as how you're in Fish Bowl, with all those windows, it won't make a difference."

"The deck, then," he says. "Fresh air."

"I brought you some cucumber slices," I say, handing him the ziplock bag.

"Awesome!" he says. "I love cucumbers."

He sets the table down and unzips the bag and eats several slices. I feel happy, redeemed.

"You want me facedown?" Dwayne asks, once he sets the table up on the deck. I suspect I am blushing. He's already pulling off his T-shirt. Sheesh, with Dwayne, Ruthanne, and Dot, I have an uninhibited group.

"Shorts, too?" he asks, hands on his waistband.

"People usually leave some clothing on, shorts or a bathing suit, if they are being massaged on the deck."

"But you need to get at my hip."

"Whatever you're comfortable with," I say as I set the sheets. Fitted sheet. Then a flat sheet. Then another flat sheet. Then the head piece. I use flannel, even in the summer, it's softer and doesn't stain as easily.

"Table's ready," I say. "I'll look out towards the lake while you climb in."

"Done," he says in a few seconds.

I give him a warmup, apply light pressure on either side of his spine to make sure everything is aligned. He smells. Burn-my-nose minty. Still better than the smelly stuff some guys put on. I'll take this mint smell over the new generation of men's deodorants — they're enough to knock a massage therapist off her Birkenstocks. Alistair used a deodorant that smelled like diesel until he got my hints that, despite what the commercials said, the smell was not a female attractant. Now, Martin, he's used the same deodorant for as long as I've known him, the same deodorant as his dad used. It smells like soap, and I like it. I wish he was using more of it this vacation. I wish he was sweating enough to require deodorant.

I know some massage therapists don't want their clients to wear any scent at all, but I don't mind so long as the smell doesn't make me gag. I don't use scented oils or lotions when I work, but it's not uncommon for athletes, especially men, to rub a menthol analgesic on a sore joint or muscle. I suspect that's what Dwayne's got going on.

"Your hip. Any other joint pain?" I ask.

"Always. My knees. My neck."

"Can you lay off the training for a few days?"

"I should do that. I know I should."

Dwayne's naked body is much as I expected. People who feel bad about their own bodies often assume that everyone else's is perfect. But a perfect body is rare. That fact makes me feel better about my own lack of a waist and my sturdy legs that were once referred to as "peasant legs" by an elderly man I was massaging. Dwayne Champion the MetaMan has stretch marks under his armpits. One of the privileges of my job is knowing these secrets about my client's bodies. I'm the only person at Happy Sands who knows about Dwayne's stretch marks. They're probably from a growth spurt as a kid, or maybe even from training his upper body.

"You're good at this," he says, when I find and diffuse a knot.

"Thank you," I say. I know I'm good at my job, but I appreciate the reinforcement.

A light breeze has kicked up. Rolling waves cover the lake, enough to limit boat traffic, but not enough to stir the sand. I look up and see Ruby at the beach. She's in the shade, lying stomach-down on her towel, reading her book. Waiting for Brie.

"Where are you from?" I ask.

"Everywhere," Dwayne says.

I hope he will say more. I could ask, is that the name of the town, Everywhere? But it's not professional to pry into a client's personal life, especially when they are working hard, as seems to be the case here, at maintaining the friendly-yet-mysterious stranger vibe.

And that's it for conversation, which is okay. Most people get quieter as the massage progresses. I glance through the window into Fish Bowl. Bottles of brand-name muscle rub line his kitchen counter. That's the smell. What's he doing with so much of it? Bathing in it?

After dinner, I take a beach walk and check on the sand version of Moby Trout. The most recent appendage has been washed away by boat waves. But also gone are the lower belly, bottom jaw, and half a tail. The pebble-eye remains intact.

I circle up toward the cabins, walking by Fish Bowl in case Dwayne has any questions about his treatment. Who am I kidding? No sign of Dwayne, but Mrs. Edwards is on her deck. She beckons me over. Just my luck.

When I get to her deck, she says, "I can barely move my neck after that so-called massage you gave me yesterday."

"Oh, no," I say. Not apologizing. The treatment I gave her should not have caused a sore neck. "Did you do anything else since the massage that could have affected your neck?"

"Of course not," she says after a pause.

I've been in this scenario with clients before. I know that during that pause Mrs. Edwards did think of another activity that might have caused her sore neck. "Perhaps sleeping on the bed or pillow in Beehive that you haven't been on since last year?" I suggest.

"I bring my own pillow," Mrs. Edwards says.

We're at an impasse. I'm not saying it was my fault. I don't believe her sore neck is related to the massage.

"Let me know how it is tomorrow," I say. "Maybe it will settle down after a good rest tonight."

"Avoiding liability, I see," Mrs. Edwards says.

Yes. And also hoping to avoid further conversation with her. I glance over my shoulder. Ruby and Brie are standing there. They each hold a badminton racquet.

"Hey, girls," I say, "Off for some badminton?"

"Do you know where the birdie is?" Ruby asks.

"I'll help you look," I say.

I wave to Mrs. Edwards and walk to the Happy Sands storage shed with the girls. It's about the size of an outhouse, with an emergency phone on the outer wall and many summers' worth of old sports junk piled inside. We dig around in the clutter but don't find a birdie. Instead, we find a small ball, and Ruby and Brie head to the beach to hit it back and forth. The ball won't wreck the racquets. They are industrial metal, probably bought at a gas station, and have been at Happy Sands for as long as we've been coming here. At about five pounds each, the racquets are more akin to murder weapons — I try not to imagine Mrs. Edwards as a target — than sports equipment, and they wouldn't be used by any real badminton player.

I drink wine on my own deck until the evening gets so dark my pouring aim is affected. There are no exterior lights at Happy Sands. Ruby comes back from the beach about half an hour later — saying the darkness ruined the badminton game and then she had a steamed milk with honey at Brie's. Of course Shelley Rocco would bring a barista machine on vacation. I listen to Ruby brush her teeth and climb into bed, her sheets receiving another layer of sand from her body. By the end of the week it will be just like she's sleeping on the beach.

Eventually I join Martin in bed and lie awake listening to the night's sounds — the soft crackle-step of a deer walking near our cabin, the low sound of television coming from Eagle's Loft and Beehive. And I hear older kids laughing on the beach. I hope Alistair is with them. He left the cabin as soon as I came in from the deck. Teens are night owls.

I roll over, put my arm around Martin. I try to think of how to help him feel better, to appreciate this holiday time, to realize that it won't be too long until our kids aren't kids anymore. I know Marty hates massage, and whenever I hint that I would like one from him, he says he doesn't know how. When Martin touches me, it's more of a pat-pat or a there-there style, like I'm a sad puppy. Which may not be therapeutic but still feels nice.

Around midnight, I hear Alistair and a girl — yes, it's Esther — talking outside our cabin. They are whispering. Then I hear Esther laugh quietly — which is surprising. Her goth mode allows only a thin-lipped smile around me, never a laugh. I hear Alistair's muffled laugh, too. Music to my ears. Isn't this what summer vacation should be about?

In previous summers, Esther and Alistair spent a lot of time together. I think there was even a romance when they were eleven. Esther couldn't sleep, probably because her mother made her go to bed ridiculously early, and so she would sneak out; Alistair had leg aches every night and would go for a walk, more like a hobble, to de-cramp. Maybe they planned the night outings in advance. I used to keep an eye on them — they were pretty young to be out roaming on their own — and hear their voices coming all the way from the beach chairs. Now I can't hear their words — they've grown stealthy — but their whispering has an excited tone. I hope they have a condom, just in case.

I spoon into Martin. He sighs. I sigh affectionately back. We weren't as young as Alistair and Esther when we met, but almost. We've been together since a Chixdiggit concert in Calgary in 1994. Martin wore a purple windbreaker and a bucket hat — which, believe it or not, was sexy at the time. We were in different high schools but ended up side by side in the stands, sharing a bottle of Southern Comfort that one of my older friends had bootlegged for me. Memory lane. I should buy some Southern Comfort. Whiskey for beginners, as we used to say. I haven't seen it in decades.

I hear Alistair and Esther come into our cabin and turn on the TV. After a while there are no sounds other than the TV. I have to pee. I don't want to interrupt them, I know they need privacy, I know they don't want to feel like I'm checking up on them, but if I don't get to the bathroom, I'll flood the bed. Alistair will be embarrassed if I go out there, especially in these baby doll pajamas. Martin would try to stop me, if he had the energy and knew what I was about to do.

I walk from the bedroom to the bathroom, eyes straight ahead, not veering my gaze towards the TV area. I pee, turning the tap on at the same time so that Alistair will not have to be humiliated by the sound of his mother's tinkle. On my way back to the bedroom, I can't help but look at them, since I am walking in their direction. Faces lit up by the TV screen, sitting on either end of the couch.

Ginny, do not sit down, I say to myself. Go back to the bedroom and close the door. Do not sit with these kids. Leave them alone. But I don't listen to myself. I sit down between them. They don't seem to mind. They seem to be mesmerized by a documentary on sharks. Maybe they are high. Oh, Ginny, what a classic mother-thought.

"Do you guys want some canary melon?" I ask.

"No," Alistair says, keeping his eyes on the TV. "It's shark week on TV."

Esther doesn't say anything. Not even a hello.

I sit for a while, staring at the TV with them, wondering how their social skills got so inadequate. They don't seem stoned. Just uninterested in me.

When a commercial comes on, I say, "I'm thinking we should arrange a bonfire tomorrow night. With everyone from all the cabins."

"Because?" Alistair asks.

"Because it's our turn to organize it," I say. "Someone takes it on every year."

"Every year," Esther says. "Every single year."

"You don't even like half the people here," Alistair says.

"That's not true," I say.

But it is true. I don't like Mrs. Edwards, for instance, but I hope Esther doesn't know that. I'm sure Alistair doesn't want to hear my spiel on community involvement and everyone doing their bit. And I don't want to admit that the bonfire is usually good for drumming up business for me. And I really don't want to admit that I wouldn't mind talking to Dwayne again. So, I say, "A bonfire is a rite of summer."

Despite their lack of enthusiasm, Alistair and Esther agree to help, probably just so I will leave. I know Ruby will help, because this will put her together with the Roccos, her preferred family.

I climb back into bed with Martin. Maybe he'll help a bit with the bonfire. A few chores might help him snap out of it. Oh, Ginny, where do you get such dumb thoughts. People don't snap out of depression. But it would make my life easier if he roused himself from this endless slumber.

It takes me longer than usual to fall asleep. I'm making a mental list of what I need to do so the bonfire runs smoothly. I'm thinking about timing and drinks and food. It's always the same food. Cheap wieners on a stick. I toy with the idea of doing something different, something that says 'firepit gourmet.' Moby Trout with some onion slices in a foil packet and cooked to perfection on the embers? Ginny, no. Okay, wieners. And booze.

DAY 4

Early the next morning, Ruby and I eat cereal on the deck in our bathing suits. I just changed into mine, Ruby slept in hers. I tell her about the bonfire.

"Are the Roccos and Oliemens coming?" she asks. She is really interested in the Roccos, of course, because of Brie, but the families go together. Like peanut butter and jam. Peas and carrots. Oil and gas.

"That's the plan," I say. "I'm going to ask them now, before my swim. Want to come?"

"Sure, maybe if they see me, they'll take me in their boat today!"

"Well, sweetie, there's lots to do around here if they don't invite you."

She sends me an exasperated look.

As soon as I see the Roccos and Oliemens heading from their cabins to their boats, Ruby and I walk over to intercept them.

"Hi, folks. Bonfire tonight!" I say, like a keen and chipper organizer rather than a person who is organizing out of a sense of duty.

"Will there be veggie dogs?" Shelley, who's closest to us, asks. Brie is already in one of the boats.

"I can pick some up," I say. Not sure why I said that. I have no desire to pick up veggie dogs. And even less of a desire to eat one.

"Veggie dogs, not tofu dogs. Tofu dogs are vile," Shelley says.

Yes, ma'am, I think. Why doesn't she bring her own veggie dogs? And what sort of self-respecting foodie eats veggie dogs, or, for that matter, any form of hotdog?

"We'll make sure there are veggie dogs," Ruby says.

"Oh, hi, Ruby," Shelley says. "You're up early. Going swimming with your mom?"

"No," Ruby says. "I've got nothing on my schedule today."

Her schedule? Ruby is talking like a middle-aged woman.

"I'll tell Brie to look you up when we get back from boating," Shelley says.

"Thanks," Ruby says. Then she does a quick little turn, and, holding her chin up and her back unnaturally straight, starts walking to our cabin.

I'd like to kill that Shelley Rocco for making Ruby feel bad. Okay, killing might be extreme. Instead, I could tamper with the veggie dogs so that Shelley gets sick enough to miss boating for a day. Okay, that's too complicated. I wouldn't do that either.

"You're welcome to come swimming with me," I call out to Ruby.

She looks over her shoulder and gives me a glare that would freeze Satan. Clearly, it's the boat or nothing. "I've got a book," Ruby says.

"Seems like Ruby's in a mood today," Shelley says. "It's the age."

No, Shelley, I want to say, it's you and your family and that stupid boat. They should ban motorboats from Happy Sands. That would fix everything.

"She reads at very high level," I say, to confirm, mostly to myself, that Ruby has a promising life ahead of her despite us not owning a motorboat. "See you at the bonfire tonight."

While I'm swimming, I decide that I'll let Esther tell her mom about the bonfire. That way, I'll avoid Mrs. Edwards and her neck. I'll stop by Eagle's Loft and tell Dot and Ruthanne. I'll

tell Kathy when I massage her this afternoon. And Dwayne —
I need to stop by his place. He wants a massage every second
day — but it's probably a good idea for me to check in and see
how he's faring after yesterday's treatment. Different people
react to massage in different ways, and sometimes buff guys
are the biggest babies in recovery. Okay, I just want to see him.
It's harmless. Nothing wrong with wanting to say hello to a fit,
cheerful guy.

I stop swimming and float, facedown, studying the
sand ripples on the bottom of the lake. I let the water do
all the work — support me, move me, fill my ears with that
comforting muted underwater sound. I spot a shadow on the
lake bottom. A fish? No, not a regular fish. I raise my head,
grab a breath, put my face back in the water. The shadow is
there again, briefly, then it flits out of my vision. Moby Trout?
No such thing.

My routine is to swim parallel to the shore until I reach
one edge of the Happy Sands property, then swim in the other
direction. This morning, I start with about ten lengths of front
crawl, then ten of breaststroke, ten of backstroke, until I hear
someone call my name. I stop, tread water. Mrs. Edwards is
on the beach. She points sharply at me and then at the beach,
indicating she needs to talk to me. Probably a complaint about
her stupid neck.

"My flamingoes?" Mrs. Edwards says as I come out of the
water. "Do you know who did this?" She points at her cabin.
I don't see the flamingoes on the lawn. Then I see some pink
in the Ponderosa Pine beside her cabin. The flamingoes are
strewn at different angles among the branches.

"This is vandalism. And I'm calling the police." She smiles
in a manner straight out of a horror movie and adds, "The
RCMP, no less."

The RCMP? Surely, the RCMP have more pressing
concerns.

"Is that a good idea?" I ask. "It's just a prank."

"The RCMP. That's who deals with vandals."

"Well," I say, "I'm sure the RCMP will want to devote all their resources to finding the prankster. What else have they got to do?"

"Maybe the prankster is the same prankster who wrecked my neck."

Oh, I see where this is going. Blame Ginny for everything. I towel off and follow Mrs. Edwards to Beehive. I might be able to reach the flamingoes and get them down for her. Case closed. Flamingo-gate will be put to rest and, at the same time, by helping her, I will have removed myself from Mrs. Edward's list of suspects.

When I get closer to Beehive, I see that all the flamingoes' necks are smashed. Who would do that? Someone who isn't a very good prankster. There's not a lot of humour in the smashed neck of a plastic flamingo. Then again, there's not a lot of humour in most pranks.

I reach into the tree to pull down a flamingo.

Mrs. Edwards grabs my arm. "Don't touch anything," she says. "That's evidence for the Mounties."

Far be it from me to tamper with a crime scene. I nod to Mrs. Edwards, cannot bring myself to say anything compassionate about the flamingoes, and head to my own cabin. I'll finish my morning swim tomorrow.

Rat's Nest is dark. Same old, same old. I fling open the fridge door, which throws a light into the room while I look for something to eat. Canary melon. Perfect. And maybe a breakfast beer with it.

"Something the matter?" Martin asks. He's on the bed, sitting up, watching me through the doorway.

"Mrs. Edward's flamingoes have been vandalized. I'm a suspect."

Martin laughs. I'm not sure he would laugh so loud if he was the suspect. But, still, a laugh is a surprise, a good surprise, coming from him.

He pushes himself out of bed, comes into the kitchen, and puts a hand on my shoulder.

"Can they be saved?" he asks.

"No. They've seen their last summer."

"Well, that's good news. I'll have a piece of melon with you," he says. "We should mark the moment."

"I was thinking a breakfast beer would mark the moment."

"It's 8:30 in the morning," he says, taking his hand off my shoulder. "At least wait until happy hour."

I wish he'd get in the holiday groove. It's not like I have beer every morning. But, on the upside, he's awake.

Not for long. After a slice of melon, Martin heads back to bed.

"Are you really that tired?" I ask, emboldened by my breakfast beer to ask a direct question.

"Yes. That's why I'm going back to bed," Martin says. "Do you need me for something?"

"Can't think of anything specific," I say.

And it's true, I can't think of anything specific. I want Martin awake during the day because it bugs me when he's sleeping. Maybe we could chat or do an activity together, like swim or write poetry to each other. I admit that writing poetry would be a stretch for us. But one time I heard a psychologist on the radio suggest it.

I decide it's time to go to Fish Bowl and invite Dwayne to the bonfire. I shower, wash my hair with the mango-scented shampoo I brought from home, and put on a T-shirt and long flowy skirt. And a necklace and some earrings. Why not? I'm on vacation. And there's someone to dress up for.

Dwayne is in a deck chair on Fish Bowl's deck. He holds a water bottle in his hand but sets it down when he sees me. He waves, and, like an old-fashioned gentleman, he stands up as I approach. What a treat to get some respect.

"Great skirt," he says. Which is a whole lot more than anyone in my family would ever say — they might not even notice I am wearing a skirt.

I give him the details about the bonfire. He says he is going to the laundromat tonight, but he'll try to make it back for the bonfire. He's only been here a few days — how much laundry could he have to do? Maybe a lot of workout clothes? Maybe I am out of touch, since Martin does all our laundry. I do know that so far here at Happy Sands, I've gone through three sets of massage sheets: Mrs. Edwards, Dwayne, plus Ruthanne and Dot, who shared. I've got three clean sets left. Usually, Martin keeps track of where I'm at sheet-wise, and replenishes the clean ones in plenty of time.

Dwayne says he's feeling okay after the massage — muscles a little tired and achy, which is standard. But I wonder if he is holding back on me because, even though I am on the grass and he is on the deck, I can smell that minty muscle rub. He must've used a litre of it. Is he still hurting? I should ask him, but I don't want to pry too much.

"Well, pop by the bonfire if you can," I say. "There will be veggie dogs along with regular food."

"Veggie dogs," he snorts. "That could be a reason to not attend."

I nod in agreement. And I think, Shelley Rocco, eat your pea-protein heart out.

No one answers my knock at Eagle's Loft. I knock again. Dot and Ruthanne's sandals are at the door.

"Dot? Ruthanne? Hello, ladies," I call, opening the door a crack. No answer.

I open the door wider. Two yoga mats, in brocade sacks, are slung over the backs of chairs at the kitchen table. I hear the shower running.

"Ruthanne? Dot?"

The bathroom door opens, and Dot sticks her head out. "What? What on earth do you want?" she says.

"Bonfire tonight," I say.

"Thanks for letting us know," Dot says, and the bathroom door clicks shut.

I close the cabin door and walk over to Beehive. Note to self: don't bother Dot and Ruthanne when they are showering. So crabby. The role of a bonfire organizer is thankless. Other note to self: plan to have a shower with someone on your vacation. It might be the secret to Dot and Ruthanne's happiness. Given their age and experience, and their lack of inhibitions on the massage table, they should probably be teaching a course in it.

I return to my Rat's Nest. Martin is sleeping. No shower for us. I grab the bag of dirty massage-table sheets from the bin in the bedroom closet. I will do the laundry myself. Illogically, I believe it will show Martin, make him feel bad, if I do my own massage laundry. Even though I am not at a critical moment of needing it to be done. I have to go to town for a few things anyway — like veggie dogs. And maybe a bottle of Southern Comfort to wash them down.

"Anybody want to come on a trip to town?" I call out.

No one responds. Alistair, like Martin, is sleeping. Ruby has gotten back into bed after the morning's Rocco encounter. She clenches the covers over her head.

"Ruby? I know you're not sleeping."

Silence. What do I care if she fakes sleep? Alistair and Martin are probably fake sleeping, too. I get a glass out of the cupboard and let the cupboard door bang shut. Then I fill the glass with water, drink, set the glass loudly on the counter. I grab my purse and the laundry bag. I let out a loud weary sigh. Ruby's tussled head appears from the bedroom.

"I'll go with you."

"Oh, sweetie," I say, "I'd love your company." And I *would* love her company. Who cares that I guilted her into it? Well played, Ginny.

We drive half an hour to the Cinderella Laundromat at the nearest town. It's a scenic drive, a view, most of the way, of Cornflower Lake, apple orchards and vineyards and fruit stands along the roadside. My mind is on Alistair and Martin sleeping back at the cabin. How can they sleep so much? Alistair could sleep till noon. Martin, in his current mode, might not be up all day. It's embarrassing to be married to someone who can't get up and trudge through the day like everyone else — even though I know I should not be embarrassed by that. I know it's not charitable.

Despite my huffiness back at the cabin, I don't actually mind going to town and doing the laundry on vacation. At home, I am glad that Martin does it all the time. In past summers, if I was by myself, I used the time to read or grocery shop, maybe take a drink in a go-cup, something light like a spritzer or a beer, and just sit in the laundromat and watch people. I'd pretend to read the paper while silently scanning people and diagnosing their physical ailments. A man limps to the dryer? He's got an Achilles issue. A woman winces when she picks up her basket? Bulging disc. An elderly woman keeps opening her hands and shaking them. Carpal Tunnel. I'm not a doctor or a physiotherapist, but I know a lot about bodies. I've had some clients for my whole career, many of them older than me, so I also have a sense of how bodies age. Twenty years from now my skin is going to be drier, thinner, less elastic — too big for my body. By then I'll probably have had at least one injury that will lead to a chronic issue, probably back related. I will benefit from more massage treatment on my own body, and my massage therapist will tell me to work on my core strength, and I will say, yes, yes indeed, I've been meaning to do exactly that.

With Ruby here, we'll likely do a tour of the town. It's a typical beach town, with a bikini shop that sells macramé bracelets, a grocery store that sells inflatable water toys, and a liquor store that sells fried chicken. And a carwash and a laundry. Here, the carwash is called Prince Charming, and it's attached to the Cinderella Laundromat.

There's no one in the laundromat, so I can't make any covert diagnoses of strangers. After I load the sheets into the washer and Ruby reads the want-ads on the bulletin board, we walk to the grocery store. I throw a couple of packs of generic wieners and one pack of veggie wieners in my basket. And buns. Martin says a good hotdog is all about the bun. We already have condiments at our cabin. I pick up marshmallows for the little kids to roast. Alistair used to roast four at a time. One for him, one for Ruby, one for Martin, and one for me. Golden brown. A sweet family moment. Maybe it only happened once. Hard to imagine it happening this year, when he'd rather not be with us. He'd rather set the marshmallows on fire.

I circle the store once more, buy some chorizo sausages and a lousy looking baguette to supplement the fridge at Rat's Nest, which is pretty well stocked with items I brought from home. The chorizo is for tomorrow, to make up for tonight's generic wieners. Alistair and Martin used to love to barbecue sausages. I'll have to tell them that chorizo is tricky. It flames easily. And tell them that they should balance the sausage with fruit and vegetables. But, baby steps. The good sausage might make them move from the couch and the bed to the barbecue. Just before the grocery checkout area, I spot a rack of summer-themed paper napkins. Sure, we need those too. Like a hole in the head. But they can double as plates. Plop. Into my basket go the ones with the smiling suns wearing sunglasses. "Summer Lovin'" they say. Sold.

Back at the Cinderella Laundromat, after putting the groceries in the car, Ruby and I move the sheets to the dryers. I read the self-help flyers and pamphlets that clutter the bulletin board. There's one on depression. I stuff that pamphlet in my purse.

A young woman, maybe twenty years old, enters the laundromat. She wears loose grey sweats with "Vancouver Whitecaps" stitched across the bum, a tight Vancouver Canucks T-shirt, and high-top basketball runners with a Toronto Raptors dinosaur claw logo on the ankle. Clearly a sports fan. Her hair is long and messy. And her face is flushed, like she has been exercising, maybe practising jumping up and down cheering for male athletes in a sports arena.

"Have you been here for long?" she asks.

"In and out," I say.

"Sorry. I'm supposed to be supervising in here," she says. "Wiping the washers and making change for people. But I had to help a friend next door at the carwash. He couldn't get the wand wash working. He uses it on his bike."

"No worries. We had everything we need," I say.

"Hi," Ruby says. "Nice runners."

Supervisor girl gives Ruby a high five.

Ruby and I fold the sheets together. She takes one end and I take the other. She holds her end high in the air, arms straight, so it doesn't touch the floor. Then I walk towards her, match the corners, and finish the final folds on my own. I load them into the laundry bag and smile to myself. Folding sheets with Ruby was a sweet moment. One of those small yet significant mother-daughter activities she'll remember when she's grown up and I'm long gone.

"She'd be a good sister," Ruby says as we leave the laundromat. I realize she's been thinking about supervisor girl the whole time we've been folding sheets. Maybe not a sweet moment.

"Based on?" I ask.

"Her runners," Ruby says.

"Perhaps not based on her job performance," I say.

Ruby shrugs. I pull into the Prince Charming car wash before we head back to Happy Sands.

"Do we have to?" Ruby asks.

"We do. Okanagan people keep their cars clean."

"We're Alberta people," Ruby says.

"We're trying to fit in," I say. "You can read on the bench over there if you want."

I put a toonie into the machine to start it, and lean into the back seat to vacuum the shrapnel from Alistair's three-day-old Timbit meal. I vacuum my way across the seat. Then, to make sure I got everything, I vacuum back towards me. There's a sharp suction sound, a yank as the vacuum ingests the bottom of my skirt. I jerk the vacuum head away from my body, my skirt remains in its circular maw. There's no off-switch on the head. And the vacuum, seemingly aware of this and empowered by the taste of cotton, sucks in the rest of my skirt except for the waistband and a small strip of fabric that does not even cover my underwear. I should have given more thought to my underwear today. I should have gone for some snug boy-cuts, perhaps in fun turquoise, instead of my loose old briefs in military white.

"Ruby!" I holler over the high-pitched suck of the skirt-eating vacuum. I need her to turn off the machine. I wave an arm at her. She looks up from her book. Confused. Still lost in the dragon story.

I'm pointing at the machine where the on/off switch is. I'm pointing at what's left of my skirt. Ruby slides her paper bookmark in her book, closes the cover, sets the book on the chair. Could she move any slower? Haven't all those dragon stories taught her to jump into action when it counts? Out of the corner of my eye I see the young woman from the Cinderella Laundromat jogging towards us. She reaches the machine, flicks the switch.

The vacuum stops.

"There you go," she says. "Why didn't you just get out of the car and turn it off yourself?"

Because I didn't think of that. I give my skirt a tug and it slides out of the vacuum.

"Thanks," I say.

"Never seen that before. Someone vacuuming up their own skirt."

Unnecessary comment, I think as I check out the material of my skirt. It looks intact. I stand up and discover the skirt material is stretched and misshapen. I am now wearing a large soft tarp.

"You coming in to do laundry?" the young woman asks. "If you wash the skirt the shape might come back."

"We just did laundry," I say, thinking she doesn't have very good face recollection.

Ruby hustles over to us. The appearance of supervisor woman a much stronger attraction than her mother's vacuuming event.

"Oh — right," the young woman says when she sees Ruby, "I recognize your daughter." Then she says to Ruby, "Hey, your mom tried to vacuum her skirt."

Ruby brings her hand to her mouth to cover her laugh. The young woman laughs. I laugh. My laugh is fake. I do recognize it's a moment to be a good sport. My skirt's not torn. Nobody died. Ho ho ho. You crack me up, Ginny.

"I'm going to stop in the liquor store," I say to Ruby once we are in the car.

"Don't you have a bunch of wine at the cabin?"

"I do, but this is not wine," I say. "It's a special drink for Dad and me."

Which is partly true. I'm going to buy that Southern Comfort. See if I can get some romance happening. And I'm also going to get some rum for piña coladas at the bonfire.

And some wine. More Pinot. We don't have enough. It's a summer holiday, after all.

Ruby and I are quiet on the drive home. I work through the urge to blame someone, other than myself, for my skirt vacuuming. Ruby is small and agile and in shorts, and could have vacuumed the backseat. Alistair spilled most of the Tim Hortons' crumbs so he should have done the vacuuming. And why doesn't Martin ever vacuum the car? I know this is a ridiculous train of thought, and that I can't blame my skirt vacuuming on anyone. But it's satisfying to mull over alternatives.

Ruby fiddles with the radio dials. I contemplate starting a conversation with her about what kind of music she likes. That seems like the type of conversation a mother and daughter should have to develop a better understanding of each other. Oh, wait, maybe I read that in a parenting magazine. Then I spot Dwayne on his bike and forget about parenting. He's riding on the shoulder. I'd recognize his back in any outfit, but it's especially easy now that he's decked out in Lycra. He's riding in the same direction we're going. It's 35°C out, he's pedalling uphill. I glance at him as we pass. He looks up. Smiles. Waves.

"That's Dwayne," I say, with perhaps too much excitement in my voice.

"Please do not stop or honk," Ruby says.

Like I would. As if.

Once we are back at Happy Sands and walking towards our cabin, Ruby carrying the baguette like a majorette, me carrying the grocery bag and the bag of sheets. I see Mrs. Edwards on her deck. She looks up from her e-reader.

"Coming to the bonfire tonight?" I call to her, continuing to walk and staying far enough away so that she can't start a neck conversation. I'm trying to work that fine line of not totally avoiding her and thereby looking like I did something wrong, but, at the same time, essentially avoiding her.

"Probably not," she calls back. "Thanks to you." She points at her neck.

Could I have hurt her neck? Did she have a pre-existing issue I don't know about? Or forgot about? I carry a notebook in my massage tote so I can take notes. But I have never used it, not once. It's not like at Prairie Physio where notetaking is part of my procedure. Next massage at Happy Sands, I must start notetaking. I tighten my grip on the laundry bag. Naw, Ginny who are you kidding. Notetaking feels like more work than the massage. Not going to happen on my vacation.

"I know you didn't hurt her neck," Ruby says quietly to me.

I give Ruby a one-armed hug. I'd say thank you, but I feel a crush of emotion in my throat, like I might cry.

Kathy's massage is in the late afternoon. She pays me in baking, a routine started a few summers ago. I was surprised when she gave me some cookies after a massage. I didn't realize she intended that for my entire payment until, well, she never paid me. Since then, the die is cast. I do like baked goods. But someday I must tell Kathy I don't do barter. I do money.

When I enter Beaver Lodge, I see a chocolate cake on Kathy's counter. It's on a plate and covered in plastic wrap, so I assume it's my payment. I try not to calculate the difference between what I could buy a cake for and what I charge for a massage.

"So, I haven't seen much of Alistair," she says, as I set up my table. "Are you sure he's all right with babysitting?"

"He's sulking a bit," I say. "But I set out that electric fishing game on the kitchen table in our cabin. Todd and Tara should be busy for a while. Alistair will keep an eye on them." I know the fishing game will last about five minutes, and then Alistair will plug Todd and Tara, and himself, into the TV. More shark shows. More shark week. Old-fashioned television is making up for the lack of internet.

"My kids can be a pain," Kathy says, "but at least they don't sulk."

Hmmm. Is that an insult? I think I'll take Alistair's sulk over some of the crap her kids do, like jumping on my massage table. I should tell Kathy about that. But I won't.

"I met the new guy," Kathy says. "Dwayne the hunk o' burning love. I wouldn't kick him out of bed for eating crackers."

"No wedding ring," I say. "Go for it." But I think to myself that Kathy is not a good match for Dwayne. I can imagine Dwayne with many women, but not Kathy. He wouldn't want a set of high-maintenance popsicle-eating twins. He needs someone who likes exercise. Someone who can help him exercise better. Like, for instance, me. And then I stop myself. Why do I care? I know nothing about Dwayne other than that he is really fit and uses too much sports rub. And he smiles a lot. And, shallow as it may be, it's nice to be around someone who smiles a lot, who says complimentary things, who pays attention.

"Sure," Kathy says. "I'll go for it. Can you massage my ass so that it looks like Shelley's or Darla's? That might help."

"No problem," I say. Kathy's not the first client to request impossible results.

We go through the established system of me standing in the bathroom while Kathy undresses and climbs between the sheets on the massage table. Kathy has a lot of anti-aging, collagen producing, exfoliating beauty concoctions on her bathroom counter. If she has enough money for all those potions, she should have enough money to pay me.

"Ready?" I call.

"Ready," Kathy calls back.

Kathy nestles her face in the head rest, and I get to work on her upper back. She relaxes well. It's not long before I hear, and feel, the classic breathing pattern of a sleeping massage client. She's tired. She needs this break.

Leaving Kathy's place, I see an RCMP officer walking towards Rat's Nest. She's tall and slim with a short asymmetrical platinum haircut poking out from under her cap. I hustle, as much as possible while carrying a massage table, to catch up to her. I'm curious, but also concerned that no one in Rat's Nest will get off their butt to answer the door. I catch her before she knocks.

"Looking for someone?" I ask. I'm sweaty, out of breath, glad to set down my table.

"Ms. Ginette Johnson," she says. "I'm told she's staying here."

"That's me," I say, slightly out of breath. "Everyone calls me Ginny."

"Sergeant Gardner," she says. "Just a few questions."

About the flamingoes, I suppose.

"Oh, sure," I say, "Do you want to come in for some iced tea?"

Why didn't I offer the sergeant water? Why offer her a refreshment at all? Is pretending I have iced tea the only way I can make myself look like a proper citizen?

"No, thanks," she says.

I gesture to a chair on the deck for Sergeant Gardner. She keeps standing, looking around the deck, her eyes lingering on the paper bag wasp nest dangling from a ceiling beam.

"Does it keep the wasps away?" she asks.

"My husband thinks so," I say. "Maybe there just aren't that many wasps this summer."

The sergeant looks disappointed, as though she was hoping for an unqualified endorsement of the paper bag.

"Okay," she says. "This will only take a few minutes. I have your name here as someone who might have information on the flamingo incident?"

"I know they were wrecked and tossed in a tree," I say.

"So where were you last night after dark?"

"On my deck, here. Having a glass of wine. Then I went to bed."

"Anyone with you on the deck? See anything suspicious?"

"Nope and nope."

I hear the window of the cabin, the one that opens onto the deck, being slowly cranked open. I can't see who is doing the cranking. Then I recognize stifled laughter. Tara and Todd, who Alistair is supposed to be watching in the cabin, are hiding behind the curtain and eavesdropping.

Sergeant Gardner looks at the opening window and raises her eyebrows in a questioning, yet tired, look that says, seriously?

I hear Alistair's voice from behind the curtain. "Hey, you guys. Get out of there."

"We're not doing anything wrong," Tara replies.

Alistair opens the curtain. Sees me and Sergeant Gardner. "Time to go home," he says. "Your mom's massage is over."

The cabin door opens, and Tara and Todd are — 'pushed' is perhaps too strong a word, I'll go with gently directed — onto the deck, and the cabin door closes swiftly behind them. They hammer on the door a few times with their little fists, then give up and trot down the deck steps and towards their cabin. There will be no need for me to ask Alistair if he enjoyed babysitting.

Sergeant Gardner smiles wanly at the backs of Tara and Todd before saying to me, "I might be back with a few more questions."

"Happy to help out," I say, although what I mean is, I'll help out if I have to.

Ruby and Martin walk around the side of the cabin. They both seem startled to see Sergeant Gardner. Ruby looks at Martin. Why would he have the answer for what Sergeant Gardner's doing here? I'm the one who's out and about.

"Hi," I say. "What have you guys been up too?"

"Tara and Todd were making us crazy in the cabin," Ruby says. "We hid around back."

"She means we enjoyed nature around back," Martin says.

"Dad napped in the shade and I read," Ruby says.

"Now that's a family that knows how to vacation," Sergeant Gardner says on her way down the steps.

I can't tell if she is being sarcastic. Regardless, I might have a drink to celebrate Martin getting out of the cabin.

An hour later, I've got my book and ballcap and sunscreen. I am beach ready. I step out of the cabin. A surreptitious glance at Beehive reveals most of the Happy Sands residents gathered there, chatting, watching Sergeant Gardner take each flamingo out of the tree and stack them in the back of her police SUV. For evidence, I guess? A few heads turn my way as I step down from the deck. If I go to the beach, I'll look like I don't care about the flamingoes, which I don't, but who beyond my family needs to know that? I turn back into the cabin. I'd even rather watch sharks on TV than go to the beach right now. Ruby, Martin, and Alistair are still in Rat's Nest, and, for a change, that doesn't bug me at this time of day. I'm glad they aren't with the herd at Beehive. Then again, they've been so glued to the television that they don't know there is a crowd at Beehive.

I turn the doorknob to reenter Rat's Nest.

"Hey, Ginny," a voice says behind me. Esther — in full dark ensemble, as usual, and appearing now, with her hood up, like an astral spirit. "Is Alistair here?"

"He's watching TV. Do you want to come in?"

"Sure," she says, following me through the doorway.

"Big show happening at your cabin," I say.

"I feel bad for my mom," Esther says. "But I won't miss the flamingoes. I don't do plastic."

I could argue the near impossibility of 'not doing' any plastics in our current universe, let alone at Happy Sands, but I don't want to rain on her impressively bold statement.

Before the sun starts to set, and before I lay everything out for the bonfire, I decide it's time to start the blender drinks. After a hot day and a flamingo investigation, not to mention several hours of dull television, there's nothing like a few piña coladas to get the party rolling. I already have the mix in my cupboard. I'm always prepared for piña coladas. But I'll need more ice. I turn to Alistair and Esther, who are doing nothing, as usual. Ruby is lying on her bed reading. Martin is asleep.

"Hey, you two," I say. "How about you go around to all the cabins and collect any ice that people can spare?"

At the very least, this ice-getting will force them to exercise their social skills. Alistair is on the couch. Esther sits beside him and keeps flipping through an Archie comic that she has pulled out from a drawer under the table.

Alistair moans, "Ice donations? Really, Mom? Door to door for ice donations?"

I remain silent. Because, really, Alistair, I do mean ice donations. And because the only retort I can think of is that maybe a good job with the ice will make up for the lousy job he did babysitting Tara and Todd. Which is not to say that those kids make for light work.

The silence extends. I can wait this out.

"Okay, okay," Alistair finally says. "We're going," he pushes himself off the couch, he holds out his hand for Esther, hauls her onto her feet. As they head out the door, I hand Alistair a bowl for the ice.

Alistair has some energy after all. I would have put up a fight when I was a teenager if my parents asked me to go door to door for anything. No, I would have done it. But I would have been full of resentment — and done a half-assed job.

I have a quick shower, which is pointless before a sandy smoky bonfire. When I am back in the kitchen, setting up the blender, Alistair and Esther return with the salad bowl half full of ice. A half-assed job.

"No one was in except the old ladies and Meta-Dwayne," Esther reports.

"His place reeks of sports rub," Alistair says.

"Do those work, Ginny?" Esther asks. "Sports rubs?"

I'm thrilled that she's asking me. I live for moments when someone believes I carry useful knowledge, thus making my career choice seem especially worthwhile.

"Menthol's a pain reliever," I say. "And some of those rubs can help with circulation, but I don't use them, and besides, they stain the sheets. Martin does my massage laundry, and he hates stains. No client wants to see a stained sheet."

I've gone on too long. Esther's attention has drifted. She gazes out the window to Beehive, where her mother is reading on the deck. Note to self, just a yes or no answer next time.

"Mom," Alistair says, "you should tell Dwayne to get off the mint stuff."

"I'll see if there's an opportunity to suggest it," I say.

"Just tell him," Alistair says.

"It's not that easy," I say.

I take the bowl from Alistair, put it in the freezer. There's not enough ice. We'll drink runny piña coladas. No one will care after the first one.

Martin continues to nap. What's new? As far as I can tell, he's only been outside the cabin three times since we arrived at Happy Sands. Oh, but who's counting? You are, Ginny. Right. So, there was the one time when the sergeant was leaving our deck and he and Ruby came around from the back. And one time when he hung up the paper bag wasp nest on the deck. And once when he was relocating a huge black beetle he found on our bedroom floor. Otherwise, Martin has been inside.

Sleeping and watching television. He could do that at home. He does do that at home. But not as consistently.

I remember the depression pamphlet — the one from the laundromat. I pull it from my purse, place it beside Martin on the bedside table. He rustles a bit but seems asleep. I give him a few minutes. Then I nudge him, remind him about the bonfire, and suggest a shower. He keeps lying there. I go back into the kitchen and fire up the ice in the blender — ha! The high-speed whir-and-clank of an over-working blender will rouse him.

While the blender runs, I practise deep diaphragmatic breaths. That's what I recommend my clients do when they are feeling stressed. I know that it's the same old story: the more I have to do, the more it bugs me that Martin is napping. And I know that most of what I have to do, I have imposed upon myself. Like this stupid bonfire.

After a couple of rounds of ice in the blender, Martin gets out of bed. Good sign. Maybe I can even get him to start the fire while I mix drinks. I'm sure I can. He's a clutch player, always there if I really need help. Well, usually there. Well, there for matters that he thinks are clutch. Or if I start to cry. I haven't cried in a while. Last time was a few years ago after I volunteered to stand in for the young male massage therapist on Alistair's swim team. Everyone loved that therapist. It's hard to be second and try to replicate what the previous therapist did. And so most of the kids were unhappy. I applied too much pressure, I didn't apply enough pressure. I was old. I was a mom. I wasn't funny. Martin stopped by the pool to see how things were going, and I burst into tears from the stress of it all. He convinced me that the swimmers and their parents were unhappy because they were doing terribly in the meet, not because of my massages.

Martin takes a long, long shower. Steam rolls out under the bathroom door. So much steam, a fog forms on the tea kettle in the kitchen. If he's trying to wash his depression down the drain, he's giving it his best effort. Eventually, he comes out in a towel, his body pink from scrubbing and hot water, face shiny as an Okanagan cherry, and continues into the bedroom. He dons clean shorts and a clean T-shirt. Then he comes into the kitchen. I kiss him on the cheek. He looks annoyed.

"I'm on vacation too," he says. "And I like to nap. If that bothers you, that's your issue. There's no need to run the blender like an alarm clock."

He takes a box of matches from the cupboard and heads outside. As he exits the cabin, I feel glad to see the backside of his righteous denial of his problem. It's not my issue. Well, okay, I've made it into my issue. I suppose a better person would ignore it. Ruby and Alistair don't seem to notice Martin's horizontal tendencies at all.

"Miz Ruby," I hear Martin say to her on the deck where she is reading. "We've got a fire to start."

I hear her hop out of her chair and say, "Yes!" That response seems over the top. I mean it is just a fire. How much fun can that be?

I spin the blender one more time, toss in some booze and some powdered mix, blend again, and pour myself a piña colada. I deserve one.

By the time I bring the first pitcher of piña coladas outside, the bonfire is blazing. Martin has done it. But the effort has taken a toll. He is slumped in a short lawn chair — the kind that's only about six inches off the ground. He seems to be staring at his knees — but that could be the shape of the lawn chair and the fact his knees are level with his head. Ruby is nowhere in sight. Probably stalking Brie Rocco. Tara and Todd are fireside, though. No sign of Kathy. The twins keep themselves busy by tossing sand into the fire. It occurs to me that Kathy must be relying on Martin to supervise Tara and Todd while she gets ready. Maybe spiffing herself up for Dwayne.

I go back to the cabin and tell Alistair he's needed by his dad at the bonfire. I don't tell him it's to watch Kathy's kids. Alistair jumps off the couch and hustles out the door. Oh, spare me. These kids will do anything if it's for their dad.

I make a couple of trips to the picnic table beside the firepit, laying out the food, setting down a stack of cups. I fan the Summer Lovin' napkins out on the table, then decide they might blow away, so I stuff them back into their original packet. I ask Martin if he'd like a drink, but he says no, maybe later. I ask Alistair, who is sitting at the picnic table ignoring the twins, if he would like a pop. He says no, and continues building a pyramid on the table with the Ponderosa Pine needles he's found on the ground.

I pour myself a large piña colada. Why not?

At dusk, Dot and Ruthanne arrive carrying more plastic cups and two large foil bags, one filled with red wine, the other with white. Both women are wearing orange tunics; I'm not sure if they are bathing suit coverups or bathrobes or dresses.

"You ladies look colourful," I say.

"Aren't these a hoot? We bought them at a yoga retreat in California," Dot says. "I feel like a Hare Krishna."

There's a kerfuffle near the fire. Todd and Tara, who have been heating marshmallow roasting-sticks in the flames, are now using them to stir up the pit and send white-hot coals everywhere. Somebody better watch those kids, I think. Not me. I look over at Alistair at the picnic table, then at Martin in his lawn chair. Neither of them seems aware that the twins are spraying burning embers. Someone's going to lose an eye, I think, and am thankful that I never said that clichéd mother warning out loud.

"Stop that," Ruthanne says to Todd and Tara. "Give me those sticks." And they do. Why didn't I just tell the kids to stop it? Maybe when I get as old as Ruthanne, I will be that efficient.

Kathy arrives a few minutes later, looking fabulous. She has her hair done in waves — she must have brought a curling iron to Happy Sands — and she wears a sleeveless sun dress. She carries a tray of tiny skewers of watermelon and feta cheese. A terrific addition to the picnic table, although, if I took a poll, I think we all would have been happier to have her skip the appetizer and instead watch her kids.

"Tara and Todd told me you had a visit from a Mountie," Kathy says.

"She was looking for information on the flamingo tragedy," I say.

"Who isn't?" Kathy says. "Those poor flamingoes — what a way to go."

Kathy makes a choking sound and winks at me. I'm not sure if the wink is a signal that she is joking, or that she thinks I am involved.

Dot and Ruthanne hand out cups to everyone except Todd and Tara.

"We're not checking for ID," Ruthanne says to Alistair as she puts the bag under her arm and squeezes it so that wine shoots into his cup. "You just holler when you need more."

I figure, go with the flow. The flow of wine, that is. This is an okay place for Alistair to have a few drinks. No driving. No dumb friends around.

The Oliemens and the Roccos and all their kids and Ruby arrive at the same time. They've come across from the Roccos' cabin, so the adults have probably been in there preloading on cocktails, building their strength to join those of us who don't own boats. The adults carry real wine glasses, and they are filled with red wine. Good wine, I imagine. There's not supposed to be glass at the beach — their wine should be in plastic cups — but it's not my job to police that. It's not my job to judge them on that either. But, oh, well, judging is in my DNA.

Ruby waves from the other side of the firepit. She looks happy standing beside Brie Rocco. No, she looks devoted, an acolyte.

"Evening, ladies and gentlemen," Ricky Rocco says. He lifts his full wine glass in a cheers motion. The Happy Sands beach slopes towards the water, and Ricky always makes a beeline for the higher side of the firepit, the side with the view of the water, and also, I suspect, the side that, due to the beach slope, makes him feel taller. Ricky is short. He wears mirror sunglasses. Right now, he's wearing them on top of his balding head.

Unlike Ricky, Doug Oliemen is tall and broad chested. He wears white loafers, hopefully only in the summer, but I wouldn't know, because that's the only time I see him. With those shoes, his boat tan, and his unbuttoned shirt, he maintains an old-time Julio Iglesias vibe. But the Oliemens and Roccos all have a perpetual holiday glow — they arrive at Happy Sands with it because they have sun holidays throughout the year. Their beach clothes are purchased while on location in Hawaii and Mexico.

"How was water skiing today?" Ruthanne asks Ricky and Doug, opening the door to a hugely boring sport report.

"We do it all," Ricky says. "Water ski, wake surf, wake board, wake skate."

I get up to refill drinks, including my own. When I get to Ruby's side of the fire, I hand her a pop.

"Whose flip-flops?" I point at her feet. Like I don't know the answer.

"Brie's," she says. "Mine broke. Brie got these in Maui."

"Broke?"

"Yeah, broke. When do we eat?"

"Soon. The coals are ready. Why don't you go check if Dwayne wants to join us?"

"What for? You already asked him."

"It's sometimes harder for a new person to join a group. How about you and Brie go over to Fish Bowl and ask him again, so he feels welcome."

Shelley, standing near Brie, throws up her arms and says, "Hey, no worries! Darla and I will go get Dwayne. It's a good way for us to meet him. And we need to fill our glasses back at the cabin anyway."

Ruthanne says, "Excellent idea. That will leave more bagged wine for the rest of us."

"Oh, didn't mean to offend anyone," Shelley says, holding her manicured hand on her heart.

"No offense taken," Ruthanne says. "It's all just booze."

"I'm empty," Darla says to Shelley. "Let's get going."

Shelley says, "You can count on us, Ginny. We will return with Dwayne."

"Thanks," I say. But I don't mean thanks. I mean drat. I can't unpack why Darla and Shelley going to get Dwayne makes me irritable. Because they are attractive? Oh, Ginny — have a drink, get over your ridiculous self. Okay, thanks, I think I will.

The kids — all the young Oliemens and Roccos, plus Tara, Todd, and Ruby — press into the table to get their hotdogs and roasting sticks. These are official two-prong roasting sticks that Happy Sands supplies. Otherwise, people, especially those who fancy themselves the outdoors-woodsman type, rip the lower branches off young trees to make roasting sticks. In our early years at Happy Sands, before the store-bought roasting sticks were available, we used unwound wire coat hangers. They were long and wobbly and hard to manage. Many wieners met their fate in the coals.

The kids circle around the fire and start roasting. I wish I had my phone so I could take a photo. This is a summer moment. Night falling, the fire casting a magical golden light across their young faces.

Alistair steps up to the hotdog table. He sets his full plastic wine cup down so he can grab four hotdogs. He attempts to skewer them all on one stick. I consider commenting on his bonfire barbarism but decide not to ruin the mood with negativity. The last hotdog slips off the roasting stick. Alistair lunges to catch it, and, in doing so, knocks over his wine cup. Wine spills across the table. He grabs a handful of the smiling-sun Summer Lovin' napkins and makes a weak effort to pat up the spill. Then he tosses the wet napkins into the fire. Billows of smoke rise as the wet napkins smother the flames.

"Oops," Alistair says to the firepit. "I thought those napkins would burn."

Thick smoke rolls over little Bart Oliemen.

"I hate dead rabbits," Bart says.

"It's not *dead* rabbits," Brie says. "It's *white* rabbits. If you want the smoke to go in another direction you have to say, 'I hate white rabbits.'"

"I hate white rabbits," Ruby says, even though the smoke is not moving in her direction.

Bart rubs his eyes. His hotdog slides off the stick and into the firepit.

"I only wanted the bun, anyway," he says.

The other kids shuffle around the smouldering fire, complaining about the smoke. I watch as they put half-cooked hotdogs into the buns.

I help the kids with condiments for their undercooked meal, and hope no one gets food poisoning. Martin helps Alistair rekindle the fire. The wet napkins eventually burn, and the fire is ready for the adults to roast a hotdog. Doug and Ricky, who have been hanging on the outside of the circle, drinking, while their children cook, take a pass. Kathy also says no thank you to a hotdog. She hands out her watermelon skewers by way of substitution. Ruthanne, Dot, Martin, and I roast wieners. Alistair cooks with us and produces three perfectly roasted hotdogs that he washes down his gullet with wine.

Esther and Mrs. Edwards arrive after dark. They have already had their dinner at the cabin. They always do on fire night. Mrs. Edwards would never cook a wienie on a stick. Esther enters the circle first, wearing a long black coat and a black toque. Perhaps she's expecting the temperature to drop. Or she's trying to blend in with the night.

Mrs. Edwards comes into the light next. She's wearing a neck brace. Good grief. I'm not asking her any questions. There is no way that the treatment I gave her could have resulted in a condition that requires a neck brace. I run through the treatment again in my mind. I did focus on her neck. I did drink a few beers before treating her. Who wouldn't? I need another drink now that she's acting like she's got the same injury as her flamingoes.

"You get rear-ended? Whiplash?" Dot asks, pointing at the neck brace.

"Feels like it," Mrs. Edwards says. She sets down a massive flashlight that she is carrying. The flashlight is the size of a toolbox. I could point out that she wouldn't carry that flashlight if she had real neck trauma, but I don't.

"Where'd you get that flashlight?" Doug Oliemen asks.

"Canadian Tire," Mrs. Edwards says.

"It's magnificent," Doug says. "Ricky, come look at the size of this thing. We need one!"

"You guys should have your wine in a plastic cup," Mrs. Edwards says to Doug and Ricky. "Go change it."

"Don't worry. We won't drop our wine glasses on the beach," Doug says. "We'll hang on tight."

Mrs. Edwards sets the flashlight down and grabs the men's wine glasses, empties the wine into two of the plastic cups I have set out, and hands the cups back to them. She does have a knack for making people obey her. Overbearing. But also effective.

A few clouds roll in, covering the quarter moon, and beyond the circle of firelight it is pitch black. Starless. When people leave the group to go back to their cabins for the bathroom or a light sweater, they can be heard stumbling, muttering, or falling and laughing.

Ruby opens a bag of marshmallows with her teeth. Probably everyone wanted s'mores. If someone dares to bring it up, I'll say I forgot the rest of the ingredients. I didn't. I hate s'mores and all their stickiness and fussiness and chocolate-y smeariness and fake Canadian-ness. Simple: that's how summer vacation should be.

Martin sits in his lawn chair most of the night, except when he gets up to add a log to the fire. Every time I look at him, it seems his chair has moved farther away from the fire and more towards our cabin. The chair exacerbates how depressed he looks. He is literally low. But he's not a total bust. When people talk to him, he responds. Sure, he responds like a man who has been flogged by life — not like a guy who is with his family and friends on a sunny summer vacation. Okay, 'friends' might be too strong a word for some of the crew here. We don't see or talk with any of these people at any other time of the year. And the main trait we have in common, besides being humans, is renting at Happy Sands at the same time. And yet, after enough years, especially when combined with massaging some of them, I do feel like I know these people. Is that friendship?

Alistair and Esther sit close together, thighs touching. Esther appears as a floating white face since her black clothing blends into the background. Upon closer inspection, I can see her pale hands and that she is pouring piña coladas for herself and Alistair. I wave, try to get Alistair's attention. He looks up. Half his face, the side closest to the fire, is lighter than the other side. I give him the throat-slash gesture. Not the flamingo one, but the that's-enough-drinking-one. Stop the piña coladas. He holds his cup up and gestures cheers.

Much later, Darla, Shelley, and Dwayne arrive at the firepit. I hear Darla Oliemen's cocktail laugh, more like a cackle, before I see them. When they come into the firelight, I see Darla and Shelley, each with a sloshing glass of wine, each with one arm looped through one of Dwayne's arms. Dwayne looks uncomfortable, which makes me feel good.

"Howdy," I say. Howdy? This Cowtown mama must have had more to drink than I thought. I try to cover it up by quickly saying, "Do you guys want a piña colada?"

"Made with a powdered mix?" Shelley asks. "I find the powdered mixes too sweet."

Oh, give me a break, I think before I take a big long gulp of my drink.

"We had some wine on the deck at Dwayne's place while we were waiting for him to show up. Then, after he got there, we had to wait for him to shower. So, we had more wine!" Darla says.

Dwayne extricates his arms from Darla and Shelley and begins introducing himself to the people he hasn't met yet.

Martin starts to get out of his lawn chair to be polite and greet Dwayne, but Dwayne says don't bother, so Martin doesn't bother.

"I hear you're training for MetaMan," Doug says when Dwayne introduces himself to him and Ricky.

"I am. Are you guys registered?" Dwayne asks, graciously, I think, since although Doug and Ricky talk a lot about sports, and still take their turns behind the boats each day, they don't look in peak condition. The term 'dad bod' comes to mind.

"Bad knees," Ricky says.

"Old rugby injury," Doug says, pointing vaguely at his shoulder.

"I'm sure it's hard to train when you have a family," Dwayne says.

Doug and Ricky nod in agreement. Yes indeed, it is the family's fault.

"You married?" Doug asks.

Dwayne laughs, "I'm married to my sport. It's all I do."

"Must be nice," Ricky says. With the implication that if only he had more time to train, he would have a body like Dwayne. And with the secondary implication that being in less than MetaMan condition is not only the fault of the family general, it is also specifically the fault of the spouse.

"Hey, Dwayne, sometime you'll have to come running with me and Darla, and give us tips," Shelley says.

"My gait needs tweaking," Darla says.

"Maybe you could set up a program for us," Shelley says. "We'd like to run a marathon."

I'm not sure how many drinks I've had, but, turns out, plenty. I blurt, "I'd be a wealthy massage therapist if I got paid a buck every time one of my forty-year-old female clients decided they had to run a marathon. Bring on the shin splints and IT band issues and —"

I feel a tug on my elbow. It's Martin. Out of his chair. Miracles do happen.

"Marty!" I shout, then take a glug from my drink and wrap my arm around his waist.

"Marty, let's party!" Ricky says.

"Hey, that rhymes!" Doug says. And he taps Ricky's wine cup with his own to acknowledge the poetic moment.

"It's getting late, Ginny," Martin says quietly, leaning over so his mouth is near my ear. "You've had enough."

Had enough? Who does he think he is? The alcohol police?

"More like you've had too little," I say quietly back to him. My intent is to be clever and funny, but, even in my current altered state, I realize I sound harsh and drunk.

"You should come to the cabin with me," he says.

"I will when I'm done here," I say. Then, to make myself sound sober and responsible, I add, "Someone has to hang around for the clean-up."

Martin doesn't look happy with me. But, well, happy doesn't seem to be his lane these days. He picks up his chair and slumps off to the cabin. Goodnight, Marty.

I scan the bonfire crowd. Darla has taken off her sandals and is balanced on one foot, showing Dwayne the bottom of her foot — apparently the perceived source of her 'gait problem.' Shelley is doing a hurdler stretch, which, in her tiny skirt, borders on lewd.

"You ski, Dwayne?" Ricky asks. He takes a step between Dwayne and Shelley.

"Cross country," Dwayne says.

"No, I mean do you water ski?"

"Never."

"How about Dougie and I take you for a pull sometime?"

"A pull?" Dwayne says.

"A ski."

"Oh. Okay. I'll give it a go."

Ruby has crossed the firepit and is standing beside me. Brie, taller, blonder, confident, stands behind Ruby like a prepubescent overlord. Okay, I might be making that overlord part up.

"Where's Dad?" Ruby asks.

"Gone to bed," I say.

I look at her feet in the flip-flops from Brie. Hers toes spread and clench with nervousness before she asks, "Can Brie sleep at our cabin tonight?"

"Maybe another night," I say. I don't want Brie reporting back to her family that Martin is depressed and that he doesn't get up with the sun in the morning.

Ruby looks downcast.

"I don't think Dad or Alistair would mind," she says. She's right. They wouldn't mind. But I mind. Brie bugs me.

"Another time," I say.

"Sometimes you're mean," Ruby says.

Well, that's a line I haven't heard from her before. This parenting business can be rough. I suppose I am mean sometimes. Who isn't?

"How about tomorrow night?" I say. "Then you and Brie can get an air mattress and sleep on the deck."

"Okay," she says, appeased. Before walking back to Brie's side, she says, "Dad and I had fun making the fire."

'Fun' Martin is not the only person who has left, but he was probably the first. Kathy is also nowhere in sight. Her kids are gone, too. Darla and Shelley are rounding up their kids, heading to their cabins. Someone, probably Dot or Ruthanne, has stacked the roasting sticks neatly beside the picnic table and started a garbage bag for the used cups and other garbage. It's not like I blacked out, but I guess I might have been getting my party on too much to notice some details? Time flies when you are bonfire-ing.

Mrs. Edwards offers a grandiose goodbye to the few people left at the firepit.

"Good evening," she says, with a flourish of her hand and a bow. And a wobble. She might have had a few drinks herself. She picks up her flashlight. "What's the matter with this thing?" she asks, flipping the switch back and forth.

"Here," Doug Oliemen takes it from her, flips the switch just like she has been doing. "Battery must be dead."

"Here, let me try," Ricky Rocco takes the flashlight and flips the same switch. "Battery must be dead."

"Here," Dwayne says. He pops open the side of the flashlight. "Look," he says, "no batteries at all."

I laugh, too long, too loud.

Doug and Ricky look kind of mad.

"Aren't you just the fix-it guy," Mrs. Edwards says to Dwayne. "Maybe you could fix my neck."

"I doubt it," Dwayne says. "Maybe Ginny can."

"Maybe if she was sober when she was working."

I wish I had wrung Mrs. Edwards' neck. First, she claims I'm a lousy massage therapist, and now I'm a drunk. What will she accuse me of next? Murder? Massage therapy is a word-of-mouth business. Do you know a good massage therapist? Why, yes, I do. Ginny Johnson. She's fabulous. Not: stay clear of Ginny Johnson. She's an incompetent booze hound.

Dwayne shrugs, says, "I had a great massage from Ginny yesterday."

He could have said more. He could have said I'm not a drunk. But at least he said something. I take a swig of my drink and look across the fire in time to catch Esther and Alistair strolling towards the beach, hand in hand. Once again, I wonder if they have condoms. I should have asked Alistair during the day. I can't exactly call out the question across the bonfire now. There's no amount of booze in my system that would make me embarrass him like that.

Before Dwayne leaves, Dot and Ruthanne load him up with the empty wine bags, the garbage bag, and a chair on each arm. Not that he seems burdened. The guy's a truck. But I was hoping he would hang out a bit, sit with me while the last of the fire burned down. And after leaving with Dot and Ruthanne, he doesn't come back. He must have an early morning workout scheduled.

I look through the fire and out to the lake. Tiny lights flicker from cabins on the opposite shore. Occasionally, a set of distant car headlights travels the far lakeside road. The lake is dead calm, not even the occasional lap of waves, and warm air still rises off the beach. I breathe in the heat, along with the quintessential summer smells of pine and campfire smoke. I reach for the piña colada pitcher.

"Want some help cleaning up?" Ruby asks.

I thought she went to bed after cornering me for the Brie sleepover. What's she doing out here again? "That's okay," I say. "I'll do it in a bit. I'm enjoying the firelight."

"Okay. I'll just take this on my way in," she says, grabbing the piña colada pitcher off the table.

"Here, take these away from me too," I say, and hand her the unopened package of veggie dogs. Not that I was going to eat them. But with the level of alcohol in my blood, I don't trust myself. I'm not a prankster, but it would be easy to become one and ruin Ruby's holiday. I'd start with the veggie dogs and Brie's mom, Shelley Rocco.

Later, when I climb into bed beside Martin, I sense that he is awake.

"Did you have a good time tonight?" I ask.

"Not really," he says. "Did you?"

"Yep," I say. But it occurs to me that I don't know if I had a good time or not.

"Want to go for a skinny dip?" I whisper.

"Maybe tomorrow," Martin says.

"Sure," I say. "Maybe you'll feel better then."

"Maybe you'll be sober then," he says. And adds, "I feel fine."

Fine. What do I have to do, tape that depression pamphlet to his forehead so he'll read it? I roll over and face the wall, lie awake thinking about how, before kids, some nights Martin and I would go to the picnic park after work and have our own bonfire, just the two of us. We'd sit on an old yoga mat and drink tea from a thermos and snuggle and talk about our days. What killed all that? Kids? Coming to Happy Sands? Bringing my job to Happy Sands?

After midnight, I hear footsteps — Alistair running out of the cabin. He's on the deck. Barfing. Everyone at Happy Sands must hear him barfing. Why didn't he go in the bathroom? My goodness, he is retching up the bottom of his diaphragm. He'll be lucky to keep his pancreas down. That'll teach him to drink too much. Natural consequences.

DAY 5

The morning after the bonfire, I'm up early, feeling dry-mouthed. I should have glugged a gallon of water before bed. I decide to swim some lengths to rehydrate my whole body. Not that I'm drinking the lake water. It's hydration by osmosis. I grab my goggles and my two-piece bathing suit. I don't look like Darla or Shelley in a two-piece. I've got a worker body. Not a complaint or a brag. Just an observance. People always bring up fingerprints as unique. But a massage therapist knows every body is unique. There are birthright features like lipomas and dimples and skin colours and textures. And imprints of the previous years the body has experienced: old surgery sites, former fractures, misalignments due to specific jobs and sports. Variety — that's one of the reasons I ended up as a massage therapist. The other reason being there was a massage school that I passed every day on my way to my brief and unhappy sojourn at a call centre for a national courier company. I need to talk to people face to face or, at the very least, as happens more often in my job, face to back.

I open the cabin door and am greeted by the smell and sight of Alistair's vomit on the deck and the railing. A magpie hops at a short distance, perhaps deciding whether the vomit is worth investigating. I return to the kitchen to fill the mop bucket with water. When I arrive back at the deck the magpie is gone, the vomit is still there.

I start to clean. So much for natural consequences. Alistair drinks too much, barfs, I clean, he sleeps in. But I don't need everyone knowing about his barf, and I don't mind cleaning it. I'm not squeamish about vomit. Human effluent is just another body function. I mean, it's not great on the rare, unfortunate, occasion when I find it on my massage table, but it doesn't make me gag. I've been known to eat a peanut butter sandwich right after changing a baby's diaper, and after washing my hands, of course.

I scan the empty beach. The empty dock. The Rocco and Oliemen ski boats float out past the swimming area. Way out. There is no movement in or around the boats, and when I squint to focus more closely, the boats look empty. Are the Roccos and Oliemens lying down in them, sleeping out there? Ginny, you are a snoop. Why, thank you. If I didn't have a hangover, I'd pour us a drink. Empty cheers.

Once the deck is clean, I head to the beach for my swim. I step into the lake, walk up to crotch depth, and then dive forward. After a few strokes, I pause, look at the boats. Still no movement within them. I breaststroke out to the nearest boat — no small task, since it is quite a way. I pause a few times en route, tread water, give myself a short break, and then resume my swim to the boat. When I get alongside, I tread water, listen. Hear nothing. So, I grab onto the edge of the boat, haul myself up the side, high enough to peek. No one aboard. This boat, and presumably the one that is floating out further in the lake, are floating on their own. During the night someone must have cut them loose.

Another prank at Happy Sands. Oliemens and Roccos would never leave their boats improperly tied. I might find the unmoored boats slightly funny if I were on the beach or at our cabin. But now, since I swam all the way out here, I have to swim all the way back. Hungover. Foggy-brained. I would have been swimming back even if someone had been in the boat. It's not like they'd invite me onboard and give me a ride. Ruby is the only person in our house with a hope of motorboat time.

It's a long swim back. When I hit the shallows, I wade the rest of the way to the shore and stand, tired and dripping, on the beach. Should I knock on the doors of Bear Den and Squirrel Nook and tell them their boats are untethered? Or shall I take the schadenfreude route and go straight for my towel, which I left on the deck at Rat's Nest? I gather my hair in a ponytail and squeeze out the excess water. A towel would be nice. Roccos and Oliemens will be getting up shortly to go boating, and they will figure out the situation themselves.

I walk back to Rat's Nest, wrap myself in my beach towel, sit on a deck chair. The doors of Bear Den and Squirrel Nook open within half an hour. The families straggle onto the beach, pointing to their boats far out in the lake. Thanks to an increasing offshore breeze, the boats have drifted even further away. The kids lose interest in the situation quickly and start playing in the sand or wandering back to their cabins. Shelley Rocco strolls back and forth on the beach in a short floral swim cover-up, until finally settling into a plastic chaise-lounge. She drinks from a big ceramic mug likely full of the latte that I wish I was drinking. Darla Oliemen, in pink pajamas bottoms and a matching pink bralette, stands at the beach end of the dock.

Doug and Ricky, in their long baggy bathing suits, are on the dock, examining the iron rings where the boats had been tied up. Then they take off their T-shirts and prepare to dive into the water.

"Hey dummies!" Darla shouts at them. "You think you are going to swim for those boats?"

Doug and Ricky turn to her.

Darla continues, "You two mopes can't swim that far."

Doug mutters something. Without Darla's volume, I can't make out the words. Darla yells, "Take the canoe!"

When there is no response, Darla adds, "Right? Right? That way you won't drown."

Doug and Ricky walk back up the dock, towards the beach. They cut wide around Darla as they head for the canoe. I would, too. She's intimidating. Does she feel good during these tirades? Does she feel good afterwards?

Doug and Ricky slide the canoe off the beach. It's the same canoe Ruby and I were in the other day. Likely not up to Doug and Ricky's usual boat standards. But still invites the question why they didn't just take the canoe first rather than make like they were going to swim to recover their boats.

The answer is soon evident. Doug and Ricky don't know how to paddle a canoe, and they aren't quick to discover the basics. They zig. They zag. Their frustrated 'switch sides' and 'paddle harder' comments to each other carry across the water to my deck. For a few minutes it is gratifying slapstick, like watching a simple task performed by the Keystone Cops or two of the three stooges. But it gets stale fast. Time to enter Rat's Nest to see my own glorious family.

And here they are — Alistair, Martin, Ruby, awake, all smushed together on the same couch, watching TV. I won't comment about the TV. At home, they would be looking at their phones. TV is slightly less annoying. And they look cute with their messy hair and TV-glare eyes.

"Who wants pancakes?" I say.

"No, thanks," Ruby says, "I ate cereal already."

"No, thanks," Martin says, "I'll eat later."

"No, thanks," Alistair says, "I'm not hungry."

I cook two pancakes for myself. A lot of work for two pancakes. I don't mention that all their eyes will be ruined from watching TV. I don't even believe their eyes will be ruined, but it's the only saying that comes to mind. I don't mention that earlier in the morning I cleaned Alistair's barf off the deck. And I don't mention that the Roccos' and Oliemens' boats are adrift. Somehow, I feel that it would ruin the moment, or the almost moment, that we are having, to bring up anything outside the cabin.

Later in the morning, the police officer with the asymmetrical hair, Sergeant Gardner, arrives at our cabin again.

"Hi, Ms. Johnson," she says.

"It's still Ginny," I say. "Ms. Johnson makes me feel like a cranky old neighbour." And here I am thinking specifically of Mrs. Edwards.

I lean against the door frame as though I've got all the time in the world, which I do. After all, I've spent the last two hours watching shark shows with my family. But time and boredom don't mean I'm relaxed when a police officer is at the door.

"Just a few questions."

"More flamingo-gate?" I ask.

"No, this is about some boats that were untied. I heard you were swimming early this morning?"

Well, isn't this a switcheroo. Someone was watching me? I bet it was Shelley Rocco in her fancy beach kimono. "I was swimming this morning," I say.

"Were the boats free floating then?"

"Yes. I was up at sunrise, and they were untied. Another prank, I guess."

"Another form of vandalism," the officer says. "Motorboats are more expensive than flamingoes. This 'prank,' as you call it, could have had large financial consequences if the boats and been lost or damaged."

Sergeant Gardner asks me the time when I was swimming, if I saw anything or anyone unusual on the beach. I tell her that I swam out to check if anyone was in them. I have to acknowledge that my idea that someone might be sleeping on the floor of the boats seems stupid in retrospect. I don't mention that my brain was, and is, malfunctioning due to a hangover. And I don't say what's the big hairy deal — Roccos and Oliemens retrieved their boats.

"So, you didn't tell the boat owners that their boats were no longer tied to the dock. You walked right past their cabins after your swim?"

"I figured they'd be awake and notice soon enough."

I won't say that I don't like the boat owners. My petty jealousies, as soothing as they are to grump about, would be embarrassing if spoken aloud. Besides, no need to offer up a motive for why I might untie the boats. Sergeant Gardner asks more questions: when did I leave the bonfire, did I go straight to my cabin, who was with me? It all seems ridiculous. Unlike the flamingoes, who now must live in a police station, the only real harm done in the boat situation was that Doug and Ricky got bawled out by Darla.

I look over the officer's shoulder and out towards the lake. I can see the Oliemens and the Roccos zipping around in their boats. Pointing towards them, I say, "Seems everything has turned out fine."

"It could have turned out a lot worse," the officer says. "Thanks for your time."

I close the door and turn to my brood and the dark innards of Rat's Nest. In contrast to the fresh air at the open door, the cabin stinks of stale coffee and un-showered family. At least someone had the consideration to turn down the TV volume while I discussed the free-run boats with the officer. This was possibly for their own benefit since I suspect they were all listening.

"How'd I do with the cop?" I ask. I lean my hips against the kitchen counter, wait for a reply.

"Good," Martin says. "I was worried you might not remember parts of last night."

Not this again. Because he's depressed, I can't have fun? And what kind of comment is that to make in front of Ruby and Alistair? Hey kids, your party-momma blacked out? Cut the overreaction, Martin.

Alistair turns the volume up on the TV. Ruby picks up an Archie comic from the coffee table.

All right then, I guess that's it for feedback and conversation.

"Anyone want to go for a walk?" I ask, pulling open the blinds to reveal another brilliant day, while at the same time, conveniently, ruining the resolution of the image on the television screen.

"No, thanks," Alistair says.

"Maybe tomorrow," Martin says.

"I'm going in the Roccos' boat," Ruby says. "Brie said she'll come by and get me."

"Fun," I say. "Don't forget sunscreen," I add, hoping I have covered up any tone or facial grimace that would indicate lack of sincerity on the 'fun' comment. What I really think is that it's too bad those boats hadn't drifted all the way across the lake. Or, better yet, sank.

I fill a glass of water, drink it, tell myself my family can't help being useless. Correct myself, they are not useless. Walk it off, Ginny. Okay, I think I will.

My walk takes me down the road that leads to the fruit stand. I wish I'd worn my runners or Birkenstocks rather than these rubber flip-flops. The sweat and swell of my feet in the heat has resulted in hot spots forming between my big toes and my second toes. My toe cleavage is on fire. Halfway to the fruit stand, I give up, turn around. And take off my flip-flops. Walking barefoot on hot pavement is not much of an improvement in comfort. Is that story about being able to fry an egg on pavement true? My feet know how the egg would feel.

I hear the soft click of a bike changing gears behind me. I step further to the side of the road to let whoever it is pass.

"Hey, Ginny," Dwayne says, rolling up beside me. He wears a tight sleeveless shirt and Lycra shorts. And a helmet.

And wrap-around glasses and lime-green cycling shoes. He's carrying the whole look off, not too obnoxious.

"Must be hot," he says, pointing to my bare feet.

"Yep. But better than in my flip-flops." I keep hobbling along, wishing he'd pass me rather than ride at my pace.

"Want a double?" he asks.

"No, thanks," I say. I'm flattered that he would ask, but I am not seeing a double. Especially on that racy bike. Especially since the last time I took a double, I was probably Ruby's age.

"Oh, come on," he says. "It'll get your feet off the road."

So, I get on. I hold my flip-flops in one hand and put my other hand under the seat — intending to hang on there — but when Dwayne starts to pedal, I lurch forward and wrap my arms around his sports-rub scented body. And it is all as truly uncomfortable and awkwardly sexual as it sounds. But also, I'm laughing.

We roll into Happy Sands like the two main characters in the final scenes of a romantic comedy: together and carefree and a little bit kooky. Except that my butt is getting sore and my adductor muscles are screaming.

Dwayne brakes and stops at Rat's Nest. I manage a clumsy dismount from his bike. The cabin door is open, and I can see the shadowy shapes of Martin and Alistair inside the cabin.

"Thanks for the ride," I say to Dwayne. "My feet would have been wrecked."

"Anything for my massage therapist," he says.

Coming from anyone else, I would consider this sarcasm.

When I enter the cabin, Martin and Alistair look at me like disappointed parents.

"What?" I ask. "What is the problem?" The exhilaration of the bike double seems to have an effect similar to booze, it's made me bold and direct with my questions.

"Really, Mom?" Alistair says. "A double from MetaMan?"

"If you guys could muster up the energy to leave the cabin, I wouldn't have to rely on the company of strangers."

Martin doesn't say anything. He turns from me to the television remote control that they have disassembled on the coffee table. He snaps two batteries into place and closes the cover.

"You've got a problem, too?" I ask.

"Nope," he says. But his curt response makes it clear that he does have a problem, not with the remote but with me. Maybe he's jealous of my double on Dwayne's bike? Too bad. I'm sure he'll sleep it off this afternoon.

"Where's Ruby?" I ask.

"Brie came by to get her," Martin says. "She's gone out in the boat with Brie's family."

Somehow the fact that Brie pulled through and did come by and get Ruby doesn't make me feel good. It makes me cranky. Lunch will help. A glass of Pinot will help. Hair of the dog, as the saying goes.

In the early afternoon, I massage Dot and Ruthanne again. They didn't book their massage for the morning since they knew they'd be out late at the bonfire and require a sleep-in.

"I had too much to drink last night," Dot says when I arrive at their cabin.

"Yes, you did," Ruthanne says. Then she turns to me, "You too, eh?"

I shrug. Older people lose their sense of proportion. They eat less, drink less, hear less. That's my sweeping generalization, and I'm sticking with it, at least for as long as these two are harping on my drinking.

"Did Martin party it up, too?" Dot asks.

"Of course not," Ruthanne says. "Martin never drinks much. But if you weren't funnelling red wine into your pie hole all night you might have noticed that Martin was, well, reserved."

Reserved. Now there's an understatement.

"Does he enjoy the bonfire night?" Dot asks.

"Oh, yes," I say. But I have a vague recollection of him telling me last night, when we were in bed, that he did not enjoy the bonfire. My sense is he just puts up with it. He once said he doesn't connect with anyone at Happy Sands. Maybe he'd like it more if he weren't depressed. Or if he drank more.

After massaging both Dot and Ruthanne, I carry my table and tote back to our cabin. I'm sweating, stinky from the walk, the bike double, and the massage. I need a dip in the lake to freshen up. I lean the massage table against our deck, too tired to stuff it in the car for storage right now. Before I get in the cabin, I hear someone calling my name. I turn, scan the beach. It's Doug Oliemen shuffling towards me through the sand. Here we go. I know, I know, I should have told them about the boats.

"Hey, Ginny," Doug says as he gets closer. He has a new hunch to his walk. His upper body tilts forward, like the middle guy in those images of the progression from bent ape to upright human.

"What are you up to right now?" he asks.

"Going swimming," I say.

"I could use a massage," he says.

Well this is unexpected. And I'm suspicious. Why a massage now, and not anytime in all the previous years? Is it a set-up for some confrontation about the boat prank?

"Maybe another time," I say, taking my bathing suit from the deck rail where it has dried since the morning.

"Last night at the bonfire, Dwayne said you gave him a great massage. And I've got this new problem." He points, unnecessarily, at his back. His problem is clear from his posture.

It seems Dwayne's testimonial has outweighed Mrs. Edwards' complaints. One compliment from MetaMan, and I am breaking new client ground: a potential massage with an Oliemen. Normally I would jump at the chance. But I need a dip in the lake.

"What do you charge?" Doug asks. "I can make it worth your while."

Oh, Doug, I think, you can't buy me.

"I'll pay you triple what you usually charge," he says.

"Deal," I say. And hang my swimsuit back on the railing.

Doug wants his massage on my deck. This is unusual, but, given the fee, and how few people come in and out of Rat's Nest, I say okay. I lug the table onto my deck and open it up.

"Just have to pop inside for clean sheets," I say.

Inside, the TV is off, finally, and Alistair and Martin are talking quietly. They stop when they see me.

"I'm going to massage Doug Oliemen on our deck. I'll be out of here in a minute, after I get the clean sheets, and you guys can resume your secret conversation."

"Okay, thanks," Martin says.

Not the response I was fishing for. I'd hoped to be included, or at least get more information.

Doug Oliemen is a big brick of a man. Big feet, big calves, thick upper body. He leaves his bathing suit on and climbs up on the table tentatively, so as not to flare his back more.

"Anything specific happen to ignite your back pain?" I ask while he struggles onto the table. "Or is it an old injury?"

I feel the stakes are high, and if I don't fix his back with this one massage, which is entirely unrealistic, I will never get a massage request from him again.

"Canoeing," he mutters into the head piece. "Someone untied our boats, and we used the canoe to retrieve them."

"Ah, that'll do it," I reply. Given how Doug and Ricky handled the canoe earlier today, I can believe that paddling caused the issue. After a few more questions, I know I'll be working on Doug's glutes and other muscles that support his SI joints.

Doug is quiet while I am working. That's fine with me. He's a hairy guy, so I mostly use compression technique and keep the top sheet between my hands and his skin. Without the sheet, I risk knotting his hairs with my hands.

After the massage, Doug gets off the table, more limber than when he got on it, thanks to my work. He hauls a wad of cash out of the pocket of his swim trunks.

"Don't tell Darla," he says. "She not a fan of massage."

"Lips are sealed," I say.

I take the money and immediately feel bad that I overcharged him. I hand him back the money except for the amount that's my regular fee.

"Are you sure?" he asks.

"I'm sure," I say.

"Thanks." He pockets the money, shakes his head, says, "The massage business must be good these days."

I'm too tired to explain that it was a moral decision, not a financial one. And his response sadly indicates that he will not be returning any of the extra money in the form of a tip. I offer a fake-gracious smile, nod goodbye and take my bathing suit from the railing before entering Rat's Nest.

Martin is in bed. Alistair is sitting upright. They both appear to be sleeping. I once heard someone say that fifty percent of the people in the world do one hundred percent of everything, the other fifty percent are well-rested. Here are two of the well-rested.

"I'm going for a swim," I announce.

"I'll come," Alistair says.

I am speechless. And thrilled. Where else but on summer vacation would Alistair come swimming with me? And for the last few days, even a swim on a summer vacation seemed a stretch for him.

I don't bother inviting Martin to come with us. Given his horizontalness, the probability of getting him ambulating, let alone swimming, is low. Alistair and I get in our swimsuits, I grab a towel, and we walk to the lake. He is bone thin, wearing a bathing suit that he's had for a few years. I understand why he didn't want to bring his form-fit jammer suit that he used on the swim team. But when I offered to buy him a new beach-style bathing suit at the beginning of summer, he said no, this one that he found at the back of his chest of drawers at home is still good. He's right, the swimsuit he is wearing is functional, still fits him at the waist, but he has grown taller since it was purchased. He brought it to Happy Sands as a statement that he didn't want to come on vacation at all. Ginny, do not comment on the too-short faded bathing suit. Be grateful that he's here. I'm trying. But, yikers, that swimsuit can't last another season.

We swim to the raft and climb on. Kathy is there, in a black one-piece, lying face down. She raises a hand by way of greeting. Tara and Todd sit on the edge of the raft. They wear life jackets and dangle their legs in the water.

"We're looking for Moby Trout," Tara says.

We've been looking for a long time," Todd says.

"Keep looking," Kathy says.

I sit beside Tara and Todd. Alistair walks to the diving board.

"Let's see a dive," I say to him. He can do a beautiful dive. Tara and Todd should see it. No, why would I think that? To show him off?

Alistair turns, smiles at me. Then, in a sudden burst he sprints to the end of the board, springs into the air and cannonballs into the water. The twins squeal when the water from Alistair's cannonball sprays up. The raft rocks madly in Alistair's wake. Todd staggers to the diving board to copy Alistair. Stops. Tara makes a bawking chicken sound.

"Any progress with Dwayne?" I ask Kathy while her kids are distracted. It's just a conversation starter; I know the answer.

"Dwayne is dead to me," Kathy says.

"That's a 'no,' then."

"I did manage to corner him for a few minutes at the bonfire, after I'd had about a thousand drinks."

"You both seem like happy people. You'd be a good couple," I say, although I don't mean it.

"I'm faking happy most of the time," Kathy says.

"Everyone's faking happy," Alistair says, as he finishes climbing up the ladder and steps back on the raft.

Alistair — my teenage downer. He dives off the raft and swims to shore. I watch him pick up my towel from a beach chair, rub his hair, wrap the towel over his shoulder and head for the cabin. I doubt he will be returning the towel to the beach for me to use.

Todd is still standing on the diving board.

"Mom," he says, in a shaky whisper. He points past his feet and into the water. "Moby Trout's down there."

He sounds scared. Kathy pushes up onto her feet and walks over to the board.

"Look," Todd points down.

"Let me see," Tara says, running to the end of the board ahead of her mother.

With the three of them, the board bows steeply toward the water. Kathy peers over her children's shoulders.

"Moby Trout!" Tara squeals. She pushes Todd off the end of the diving board. He screams like he's been thrown into a pool of piranhas. Tara jumps in after him.

"That's enough," Kathy says as she tries to steady herself on the rebounding board. She carefully turns, takes a few steps.

"Was there a fish?" I ask.

"I doubt it," she says.

I peer into the water. It's deep green-black and choppy from Tara and Todd. They kick circles around the raft, the life jackets making them swim like splashy tubs. Moby Trout would be a fool to stick around this scene.

Kathy walks to the ladder, descends into the water.

"Kids, let's go in for a snack," she calls to Tara and Todd. Then she says to me, "See you in a bit, Ginny. I'm going to see if I can trick these guys into a nap."

"Good plan," I say. Martin could teach them how to nap.

"Enjoy your alone time," she says.

Like I need more alone time. I try to visualize myself as the woman on a serenity card. Woman basking on raft. I lie on my back. The warm sun and the gentle rocking should be peaceful. But no. It's too hot. I'm sweating. Uncomfortable. How do people suntan? I roll onto my stomach. Look across the water. In the distance, a boat speeds by, pulling a skier on two skis. The skier's posture is that of a beginner — shoulders and arms forward, bum sticking out. The boat changes course and soon I see and hear it speeding towards Happy Sands, towards me. Not as the crow flies, though, more in a wide zig zag pattern. Odd, even cartoonish, for a boat pulling a skier. In my imagination I hear the song "Yakety Sax." When the boat is almost at the raft, it turns and tows the skier parallel to the shoreline. For a moment it zooms out of sight, then it comes roaring back in front of the raft again. The boat does a quick U-turn and the skier is whipped off the rope. He stays on the skis for a moment, his arms start to circle wildly as he loses balance and crashes backwards on his bum. He sinks for a few seconds, then he pops out of the water, gasping, and the skis pop up beside him. Hello, Dwayne.

The boat has slowed down and pulls into the Happy Sands dock. Ricky Rocco is driving. Doug Oliemen is riding shotgun. Doug's back must be feeling better for him to be in a boat. I certainly wouldn't have prescribed a wild ride in a motorboat immediately after a massage.

96

"Perfect water for skiing," I say to Dwayne after I stand up on the raft.

"I think they were trying to kill me," he says. "They kept driving me around and around. My arms are poached. I'm glad I've got a massage booked with you tomorrow."

Seems Doug and Ricky are unhappy about a new jock on the beach.

"You should put some ice on those forearms right away," I call as Dwayne starts swimming to shore, pushing the skis ahead of him.

"You got all my ice last night for your piña coladas. I'll use some muscle liniment."

Sure, like he needs more liniment.

A few minutes later — I don't want to look like I am following Dwayne — I swim to the beach. I feel this morning's long swim in my aching muscles. A shot of Southern Comfort on the deck will fix me up in no time.

As I walk to the cabin, dripping, thanks to Alistair's towel theft, Ruby and Brie run up to me.

"So, Brie is sleeping over tonight? Right?" Ruby says, more of a confirmation than a question.

"You bet," I say. "Ask Dot and Ruthanne if you can borrow their air mattresses to sleep on."

"Oh, we have lots of air mattresses," Brie says.

"Super," I say. "Use those."

Of course the Roccos have lots of air mattresses. Ginny, there is no reason for that to bug you. But it does.

When I get to Rat's Nest I pour myself that shot of Southern Comfort. Alistair and Martin are looking at me. I guess I should ask them if they want anything. But, wait, why should I? I'm on vacation. I put half of Kathy's chocolate cake on a plate, get a fork, refill my glass with Southern Comfort, and take it all out on the deck to enjoy. Good for you, Ginny. Relax. Thanks. I think I will.

I settle into my chair, eat cake, drink, wonder how Dwayne's strained forearms are doing. I can help a bit when I massage him tomorrow, but it's going to take a few days before he feels back to normal.

The cabin door opens. Martin and Alistair step outside, each with a piece of cake on a plate.

"Want company?" Martin asks.

"Sure," I say. "It's happy hour."

"We like the idea of cake for happy hour," Alistair says. I get the implication — they don't like the idea of Southern Comfort for happy hour.

We eat cake, watch the lake. The scene is perfect, except Ruby is not here. And then, like holiday magic, here she comes, jogging up from Squirrel Nook.

"I'm getting more cake," Alistair says, getting out of his chair. As he heads into the cabin he adds, "I earned it, babysitting Tara and Todd."

"How's your hangover?" Martin asks me, while Alistair is in the house and before Ruby reaches the deck.

My hangover? Well there goes the happy hour. I still have a slight headache, but it's not like it has held me back from work today. I massaged Ruthanne, Dot, and Doug. So, I don't know that the interrogation is relevant.

"If you want to worry about a hangover," I say, "I think you should worry about Alistair's. He barfed all over the deck last night."

"He told me," Martin says.

Do the kids tell Martin everything?

"Hi, guys," Ruby says, hopping onto the deck. "Can we eat dinner soon? Brie is coming over."

Alistair appears with his second piece of cake.

"Can I have some?" Ruby asks.

"There's none left," Alistair says.

Ruby looks at me as if to ask, Is he right? None for me?

"Here, you can have this," Alistair says. He hands Ruby his plate with the last piece of cake on it.

That's kind. I should tell him. But I won't. Not now, anyway. There doesn't need to be a huge celebration every time someone does a good deed.

After the cake, I feel nauseous. It might be the cake and Southern Comfort layered on top of the long day, layered on top of a hangover. Or it might just be the cake. I decide to lie down in the bedroom for a few minutes before making dinner. Who wants dinner right after cake? Maybe a salad. Later.

I stand up.

"Where are you going?" Martin asks.

"For a drink," I say. Because I know that is his concern. I wait a few seconds, and, for clarity, I add, "of water."

I walk in the cabin, make a sharp turn into the bedroom. I'll lie down for a few moments.

Hours later. The bedroom is almost dark. Someone jostles my shoulder. Martin. There he is, leaning over me. I remember where I am. Happy Sands.

"What time is it?" I ask.

"After ten," Martin says. "Nighttime."

I sit up. Let my eyes adjust to the light and let my brain adjust to the fact that I've been sound asleep.

"Were you having a nap?" Martin asks, smiling wryly as he sits on the bed beside me. I should be a sport, accept the gentle kidding, and say I had a nap. I had a terrific nap — the first I can remember in my adult life. But do I have to eat crow immediately after waking up?

"No," I say. "I don't nap."

"Gotcha," he says.

Martin has taken care of everything while I slept. He fed dinner to Alistair and Ruby, and, also, to Esther and Brie. He helped Ruby and Brie set up their sleep space on the deck, pulling the sheets off Ruby's bed and setting them up on the mattresses.

To make room on the deck, Martin has brought my massage table inside.

"I couldn't find the car keys," Martin says when he sees me stepping around the table as I make my way out of the bedroom. "Otherwise I would have put it in the car."

"No worries," I say. "I'll do it in the morning."

"Can you close the door?" he asks. "I'm going to call it a night."

I shut the door. Imagine him climbing into the spot in the bed that I just left. I can't be bitter about that. It's not a totally unreasonable time to tuck in for the evening.

Alistair and Esther are on the couch. Watching TV. Alistair is in a long sleeved shirt and jeans, Esther is in her chain pants and a black flannel shirt. The barely clad beach scene is not for them.

"Hi, Mom," Alistair says, "We played badminton when you were napping."

"I wasn't napping," I say. Not sure why I am carrying on this no-nap charade, but I am in the groove now.

"We stopped because Esther hurt her shoulder," Alistair says.

Esther demonstrates by showing she how far she can raise her arm — not quite to shoulder height.

"Can you fix it?" Alistair asks.

Aha. I am useful for something. I have this massage skill.

"Maybe," I say. "I'll have to take a look."

"I'll open your table," Alistair says, springing off the couch, full of energy for Esther.

Esther's eyes dart around the room in panic. Probably because her mother is claiming my treatment ruined her neck. But her panic might be triggered by more than that. I remember Esther saying that she doesn't like to be touched by people. Although, judging from their cuddle position on the couch, it seems that Alistair might be an exception to her definition of people.

"Only if Esther wants," I say. Then add, "And, Esther, you can lie on the table with all your clothes on. It doesn't have to be a big deal."

"I'll try it for a minute," she says.

A minute treatment isn't going to help. But we'll proceed with baby steps. Esther gets on the table, face up, arms tight to her sides, her body stiff as a tin soldier. I ask her a few questions, try to make her feel at ease. I softly touch her arm and her shoulder. Tell her what I am doing before I do it. It seems she has a mild rotator cuff injury. She agrees to roll onto her front. I work her shoulder, mainly her supraspinatus muscle. Lightly. Bad enough that her mother is wearing a neck brace, I don't need to risk adding to Esther's inflammation and having her appear tomorrow in an arm sling.

Esther's flannel shirt rides up as I work, and I notice she's got a dimple piercing on her lower back. Two tiny silver baubles on either side of her lumbar spine. The site looks healthy. I wouldn't be concerned about working in the area. Even though she has a shoulder injury, I'd like to work the whole back to catch the interrelated muscles. For Esther's comfort, though, I will keep to her clothed shoulder.

I've seen several back piercings on clients. If I see one that is not fully healed or showing signs of infection, I won't do a massage. One of my clients has a nape piercing, two red gemstones on either side her spine at the back of her neck. It reminds me of a misplaced vampire bite, but that might be the artistic intention. And I have seen one barbell piercing on a client's back, low down, right about where Esther's dimple piercings are. It was easy to work around.

Esther must sense I am looking at her piercing. She reaches around with one arm and tugs her shirt towards her pants.

"Don't tell my mom," she says.

"I can't tell anyone. That would be professional misconduct," I say. "Not that I'd tell anyone anyway."

Esther releases her grip on her shirt, brings her arm back to table.

"I want to tell you about my mom's neck," she says into the face cradle.

"Is it still sore?" I ask.

"I think it's from being on her e-reader all the time."

"That's a possibility."

"My mom isn't really mean. She's just jealous of you and your perfect family."

"Me?"

"All happy and doing things together."

"Us?" I can't think of anything we've all done together on this vacation. Oh, watched television.

"Well, I know your family is not perfect," Esther says. "Like, obviously. But there's no convincing my mom."

Obviously.

I'd like to work longer on Esther, but I better leave it at half an hour. Her shoulder has taken the treatment well. Her breath is relaxed. I give her a light pat on the back and say, "All done. You can stay on the table for as long as you like."

Esther gives me a thumbs-up. Alistair gives me two thumbs-up. My work here is done.

I walk to the front door, stick my head out to check on Ruby and Brie. I watch them for a while to make sure they are truly asleep and not pretending. No stirring or muffled giggles. It's a warm night, even by Okanagan standards, with a small lap coming from the lake, a rustle of the long-needled Ponderosa pines. Also, there's the soft rattle of Martin's paper bag faux-wasp nest as it bumps and swings in the wind. Oh, and there's the overriding sound of the TV coming from within our cabin. Close to perfect.

I return inside. Esther still lies face-down on the massage table. She might be asleep. Alistair, still on the couch, also might be sleeping. It seems weird for me to be in the room with this sleeping duo. Not so weird that I don't take the time to turn off the TV. Then I join Martin in our bedroom. I softly shut the door behind me, change into my baby dolls, crawl into bed. Martin wraps an arm around my waist. I close my hand over his. Let our perfect vacation begin. Maybe Mrs. Edwards is onto something.

DAY 6

I wake up at three a.m. My first thought — what have I done, allowing Ruby and Brie to sleep on the deck? Two recent nighttime pranks and two visits from Sergeant Gardner weren't enough to indicate to me that little kids should be inside at night? My other thought — where is Martin? I run my hand across his side of the bed, an unnecessary gesture, since he could not be hidden in the flat swirl of sheets. I get out of bed, open the bedroom door. Lo and behold, there is Martin, in a pair of white boxers, on my massage table. He's on his stomach, resting on his elbows. In his hands: his telephone. I press my own hands onto the top of my head to keep my lid from blowing off.

So much for no telephones at Happy Sands.

More disturbing is how intently he is using his phone. He has no idea I am standing beside the table. I look at his screen. Candy Crush! That's what he's spending his time on? That stupid puzzle game.

Martin's thumbs stop moving. He turns to me, opening his eyes wide and trying to give me a cute caught-with-my-hand-in-the-cookie-jar look. He is much too old, and I am too irritated, for that look to succeed in diffusing the situation.

"I have insomnia," he says. "This helps."

I suspect phone games at three a.m. might be part of the cause, not the cure, for insomnia.

"Here," he says, handing me the phone. "You better keep it."

"Why didn't you leave your phone at home?"

He shrugs. "I was almost at a new level the day we left."

I take the phone. Wonder how much of our family data plan he has used up playing Candy Crush here at Happy Sands.

"I got the new level," he says.

Whoop de do. I can't bring myself to ask how he managed to get his phone back from our kitchen table at home after we'd all set them down there together. And I can't bring myself to ask if he's been playing Candy Crush every night we've been here. While I'm sleeping. It's like he's been having an affair with Candy Crush. I already have more information than I want. And I don't want to fill in the sordid details.

Martin climbs off the massage table and goes into the bedroom. He is not walking sheepishly enough for me. He has not apologized. He *is* like a kid caught at the cookie jar.

I close up the massage table, lean it against the wall. On my way to the door to check the girls, I walk past the bedroom where Alistair is soundly sleeping. He has one long leg wrapped outside the sheets, hanging off the end of the bed. And one long armed splayed across the bed and hanging off the side. This boy can sleep.

I open the front door and peek at the deck sleepers. All is well. No sign of pranks. But I know I won't be able to go back to sleep while these girls are out here on their own. I walk to the beach, grab a plastic chaise lounge, drag it up to Rat's Nest, stopping in front of the deck. I'll rest here till daylight. It will serve the dual purpose of watching over the girls, and, by not going to my own bed, of showing Martin exactly how mad I am about the phone.

Turns out, after an hour or so, there is no real rest to be had in a plastic lounger. The cross-slats dig into my back and legs. The armrests are too high and sharp edged to be suitable for my arms, or, I think, any human arms. And even though the evening is warm, the plastic feels cold and damp. I lie awake, wondering about people who claim to be relaxed, rested, reenergized after summer vacation. My sleep cycle is entirely disrupted. I went to bed at six p.m., Martin woke me up at ten p.m., I went back to bed at midnight, I woke up at three a.m. to find him on his phone, and here I am outside on a lounger at sunrise.

When I finally hear the girls stirring, I slip into the house and start to make them breakfast. Ha, I'll show that Shelley Rocco that I am the Queen of the Pancake.

I'm not surprised that Martin and Alistair are still sleeping. Alistair and Esther were up late. I went to bed before Esther left. And Martin must surely be exhausted from his Candy Crush-ing. Lack of sleep, caused by gaming in the wee hours, is probably the source of his depression. Oh, Ginny, you're too smart to draw that conclusion. Yep, I know. But it feels good to draw a straight line to a conclusion with no consideration for other factors. Keep the straight line to yourself. Will do.

I whip up my finest batch of pancakes. Fluffy with fresh blueberries. Maybe not foodie-food, but definitely Calgary comfort food. When Ruby and Brie wander into the cabin from their deck sleepover, they are met with a pancake tower, and, for the record, real maple syrup, not a sugar-water imposter. Ruby smiles broadly. I have done it. I have made that smile with these pancakes. Ginny, you are a genius.

"My mom said I couldn't sleep on your deck," Brie says as she pulls her chair to the table.

I'm not sure how to respond. The words 'fait accompli,' come to mind, but I am not confident in their meaning or in the point of saying them aloud to two pre-teens.

Brie piles three pancakes onto her plate. Reaches for the syrup.

"She said I could only sleep over if we were inside the cabin. Because of the prankster," Brie says.

Ruby looks at me with worried eyes. Rightly guessing this is where her perfect sleepover could go sideways.

"These are good pancakes," Brie says. "I'll tell my mom you slept in that chair beside us all night."

Far be it from me to inquire whether Brie thinks I was out there all night, or if she knows I was only there for the early morning hours. But, also, far be it from me to say thank you. I have the sense that if the pancakes weren't to her liking, she would have thrown me under the Shelley bus.

After Ruby and Brie head to the beach to play, and I've done all the dishes, I decide it is time to indulge in a breakfast beer. I can hear Martin moving in the bedroom, and if he sees me with a beer, he will not approve. What do I care if Mr. Candy Crush approves of me? He was so busy disapproving of the Southern Comfort I had with my cake last night, making his usual sour, pinched-mouth, expression every time I poured myself a drink, that I never got around to telling him I bought it after reminiscing about when we got together.

I pop open a can of beer, pour half into an empty coffee mug, top it off with some tomato juice. A Calgary Red Eye. It's in keeping, at least at some morning parties, with the pancake breakfast. I take my mug out to the deck. Before I settle into a chair, I open the plugs on the air mattresses. Air seeps out in a sad whistle. Bottoms up, Ginny.

Red Eyes are easy to drink. Clam Eyes, with clamato substituted for tomato, not so much, at least early in the morning. Clams and mornings should never be combined. I finish my Red Eye and have time to go in the cabin and make a second, and get back to the deck, before Martin is fully out of bed. He pads out to the deck in bare feet and an old disintegrating pair of gym shorts. He holds two coffees.

"Morning," he says. "I brought you a coffee."

"I see that," I say. I'll let him sweat the phone episode for a while. So far, the guilt has been positive. He is outside and has brought me a coffee.

"Sorry about the phone," he says. He waves to Ruby at the beach, which leads me think he is not too focused or invested in the apology.

"Did you have a good sleep?" he asks.

"I slept in a lounge chair in front of the deck."

"Oh, I didn't notice. What did you do that for?"

If I say my reasons aloud, they will sound stupid. So, I say nothing. Instead, I look at his bare chest. He used to have a smattering of freckles across his collarbone. Now I can't see them. Maybe it's the light on the deck that makes them hard to see, or maybe they have faded from lack of sun. My bet is on the latter, given Martin's outdoor activity level so far this vacation.

We drink coffee in silence and watch Ruby and Brie playing a game at the beach. The concept of the game is unclear, but an element of long jump is involved. Ruby is smaller, but quick and lithe. She jumps further every time. Her competitiveness prevents her from noticing that Brie is not enjoying losing every set.

"Refill?" Martin asks.

"I have to work this morning," I say. "Only one coffee for me." As usual, I have to watch my fluid intake. Also, even before the coffee, the Red Eyes had my bladder near capacity.

Roccos and Oliemens appear from their cabins, start to get their boats ready at the dock. Brie runs over to her family. I'm guessing Ruby, having shown off all morning, will not be in the Rocco's motorboat plans today.

Alistair joins us on the deck. Sinks into one of the plastic chairs, as much as anyone can sink into a stiff plastic chair.

"I hope Esther's shoulder is better," he says.

"Might take a while," I say.

"How many days do we have left here?" Alistair asks.

"Two. Today and tomorrow. We leave early the morning after that." For me, enough time for a few more swims, a few more cocktails, maybe one more massage with Dwayne after today. Gotta get him Meta ready.

"Is that all?" Alistair asks. He has forgotten that he didn't want to accompany us on vacation. Thank you, Esther. I refrain from suggesting that he might not want to waste those two days on shark shows.

I head inside. Shower. Dress. Check my tote for clean sheets. I approach my massage table, try to not think of Martin playing Candy Crush on it in his underwear. What has been seen cannot be unseen. I grab the handle, hoist and carry the table out of the cabin.

"See you later," Martin says from the deck.

"Bye, Mom," Alistair says.

I don't reply. Might be nice if they offered to carry the table for me. Not that I can't carry it myself.

I walk barefoot, with the table, to Fish Bowl. The sand has heated up enough to make me step quickly. Ever since my flip-flops wrecked my feet, I've been shoeless. My heels have become dry and cracked from the sand and the heat. People talk about the physical benefits of walking in sand — it strengthens the foot and leg muscles and delivers an ersatz reflexology treatment. No one seems to talk about how dry Okanagan sand, we're not talking spa mud here, turns your feet into hooves.

Dwayne's ready and helpful as always, taking care of one side of the table as I unfold it and set the sheets. While he pulls off his shorts and hops onto the table and into the sheets, I look out over the deck to the water, scan the beach for Ruby. I see her on the boat dock, alone. The boats have left without her.

"Ready," Dwayne says.

I turn my attention from Ruby to Dwayne. I adjust his arms so that they are outside the sheet. Concentrate on the massage, Ginny. I lift one of Dwayne's arms. Work through the layer of sports rub he's applied and use my thumb and fingers to treat his extensors with effleurage. His forearm feels like a giant ham hock. Waterskiing with Ricky and Doug has done a number on him. And I notice he has a rash on his forearms — possibly from the heat but more likely from all the sports rub he has applied.

"I'll come back to your forearms," I say, moving to the end of the table and starting on one of his feet. Best to get the rest of the body done before I tackle those forearms. He has stocky feet, thick, with good arches. I work the sole, the calf. I look out across the lake again and see the Rocco and Oliemen boats, full with their people, hooked together. I can see kids jumping off the boats, having a swim. Because sound travels so well across water, I can hear their happy hollers. Ruby must be witnessing it all, too.

I start working on Dwayne's hamstrings. Runner's hamstrings are usually tight. Effleurage first. Then some kneading. I try not to let my thoughts about Ruby and the boats result in overly vigorous kneading. Breathe, Ginny.

But my mind is scattered. I hear the swish-swish of bird wings. Pay attention to the massage, Ginny. I hear the bird wings again and look up. A raven circles near the Fish Bowl deck with something oblong in its mouth. Part of a baguette. From my house? I bought a baguette the other day. What are the odds. I glance over at Rat's Nest and see a flash of orange. Fire. In the barbecue. Alistair and Martin — those idiots.

"Dwayne, I'm sorry, I know this is totally unprofessional, but I have to leave you on the table for a few minutes to run back to my cabin."

"No problem. Anything wrong?"

"Just need to check that the barbecue is off at my place."

"Take your time. I'm happy to lie here. Must be the waterskiing — I've never felt this exhausted."

The flames in the barbecue are subsiding as I run up to Rat's Nest, but I figure I may as well keep going to make sure there are no more flare ups. It would take nothing for the wood cabin to catch fire. When I get to the deck, I see several red-hot glowing objects in the open grill. The chorizo sausages. Burnt to a crisp.

"Alistair? Martin?" I call as I turn off the gas to the barbecue.

No response. I look around. See two plates on the railing. One with half a baguette. One empty. That would be the raven's plate?

"Alistair? Martin?" I call again.

I step into the cabin. Don't see anyone. I hear someone in the bathroom. "Hello?" I ask the bathroom door.

"What?" Martin answers from inside.

"There was a two-storey blaze on the barbecue."

An exaggeration on my part. Any fire at all should be enough for concern. But I am feeling dumb that I have left Dwayne on the massage table for charred chorizo on the barbecue. This would never happen in my office at Prairie Physiotherapy.

"That's Alistair," Martin says. "He went to get Esther. He's making them lunch."

"He just about burned the whole place down."

"I'll be out in a second."

"Never mind," I say. "I have to get back to work." Back to Dwayne. Back to normalcy.

I jog back to Fish Bowl. I need to settle my mind, get in my massage zone. But even before I reach the deck, I notice that Dwayne is no longer on the massage table. He wasn't that tired after all? Maybe he's getting a drink of water? Dwayne, please don't be applying more sports rub.

"Apologies for the interruption," I say loudly, so he'll know I'm back. "I never leave a client on the table — not unless I think a building is about to burn down." I peer through the glass into his cabin. No one in there. I'll wait. Maybe he's in the bedroom or the washroom.

I examine my table. Where's the top sheet? Sometimes it falls on the floor when clients leave the table. I lean over the table to check for the sheet — and see Dwayne's still body on the floor, behind the table, the top sheet tangled around his lower torso and legs.

"Dwayne?"

No response.

I hurry around the table to the side he is on, get on my knees. Touch his shoulder. Put my ear to his face. Listen for breathing. He's breathing. But not conscious.

Think, Ginny, think.

I take a quick look up. I see Alistair coming out of Beehive with Esther.

"Alistair!" I yell. "Call 911 on the emergency phone."

"What?" Alistair yells back.

"Call an ambulance."

"What emergency phone?" Alistair says.

He'll have to figure it out. I can't waste time yelling instructions. I have to do something, anything, for Dwayne. I use my hands to lightly probe around Dwayne's body looking for clues. I'm shaking. What has happened to him? Fell getting off the table? Had a stroke? That seems unlikely. Focus, Ginny. I close my eyes, try to calm my thumping heart. When I open my eyes, Alistair is on the deck.

"I don't know where the emergency phone is," he says.

"In the storage shed," I say. Then I remember Martin's phone. "Dad's phone is in my underwear drawer at the cabin."

"He's got his phone here?" Alistair says. "How come he gets a phone?"

"Not now. Alistair."

My sharp tone activates Alistair. He leaps off the deck. I hear his first few steps as he runs in the sand.

I check Dwayne's pulse. I scan his body. I do the first aid ABCs again. Airway not blocked. Breathing is normal. Circulation seems fine with no signs of bleeding. I'm at a loss about what to do next. I'm a massage therapist, not an ER doctor.

I feel Martin beside me. I'm kneeling on the floor and see his long pale feet before he crouches, and I see his face. He knows less first aid than me, he's never even taken a course, but I am thankful to have him at my side.

"We called an ambulance," he says. "What happened?"

"I don't know."

Martin leans in, listens for Dwayne's breath. Looks at me. I must look a mess because his eyes soften. He takes my hand and says, "It'll be all right, Ginny."

Martin holds my hand until an ambulance, lights flashing, drives through the sandy central area of the cabins and pulls up in front of Fish Bowl. Two paramedics get out. When they reach us, they tell Martin and me to move back. It's a relief to unload responsibility to them. They examine Dwayne while they ask me questions. One of the paramedics returns to the ambulance and pulls out a wheeled stretcher.

"Does this man have any family here?" he asks.

"No," I say. I squeeze Martin's hand. I am glad to have him here.

A police cruiser, lights flashing, pulls up. Sergeant Gardner steps out of the vehicle and talks with the paramedics. She walks up the steps to Fish Bowl and gives me a nod. Not a friendly 'hello again' nod — more of a this-is-serious nod.

A crowd of Happy Sands people has gathered a few metres from the deck of Fish Bowl. I look anywhere except at those people.

"Why don't you all go for a swim?" Sergeant Gardner says to them.

"Mom?" I hear Ruby call out. For Ruby's sake, I'll look at the crowd. She is in the front, looking small and scared.

"What's happening?" she asks.

"Your mom is okay," Martin says.

"Come with me and Esther," Alistair says. They are on the outskirts of the crowd, too. Alistair beckons to Ruby to come with them as they start to walk to Rat's Nest.

Dwayne moans when the paramedics lift him onto the stretcher. Any sound at all from him is a positive to me. Even though his vital signs indicated he was alive, without any sound from him I couldn't shake the fear that he was dead. When the paramedics carry him down the deck steps, the wind kicks up and the sheet slips off the bottom half of his body. One of the paramedics picks up the sheet and plops it over Dwayne's crotch. They wheel him into the back of their vehicle, close the doors. Lights flashing, they drive away slowly, allowing the crowd to part and let them through.

Sergeant Gardner asks me questions. Many are the same as those asked by the paramedics. Did Dwayne mention any body issues before the massage? How long was I away from the table? I answer truthfully. I can't hide the fact that I left him on the table.

"That's probably enough information for now," Sergeant Gardner says. "I want to take a look inside Mr. Champion's cabin."

"Should I take my table?" I ask.

"The table stays right where it is," the sergeant says.

"Probably for the best," Martin says to me. And he's right. I'm in no state to massage anyone. And who is going to want a massage from me after this anyway?

Martin and I walk towards our cabin. Some of the Happy Sands spectators have drifted to the firepit. There's no way to avoid them.

"Hey, Ginny," Doug Oliemen calls from the group, "What did you do to Dwayne?"

"Nothing," Martin says.

"That's not how it looks," Oliemen says, coming closer. When he is close enough to only be heard by us, and not the group, he says, "I didn't know I was risking my life when I had that massage from you."

Martin says, "Give it rest, Doug." And we continue walking to Rat's Nest.

Once we are inside our cabin, and have closed the door, I ask Martin, "Do you think I did something wrong?"

"No." He pauses, then asks, "Do you?"

"No," I say. But without confidence. I am shaken. Bodies are complicated. Maybe I missed a symptom. Maybe I triggered a reaction.

Martin says, "Even if alcohol played a role, you couldn't do that to someone."

Even if alcohol played a role? I think about that. Take the glass of tap water that Martin offers me. Drink it slowly.

Alistair and Esther and Ruby are in the kids' bedroom. They have set the fishing game up on one of the beds.

"Hey, guys," I say. I make an effort to sound normal, if not chipper, but I can't think of anything more to say.

"Everyone feeling okay?" Martin asks.

"Okay," Alistair says.

Esther and Ruby concentrate on trying to catch a fish with the tiny magnetic rods.

"Is Dwayne dead?" Alistair asks.

"No," I say. "I don't know what's wrong with him."

Alistair's eyes fill with tears. "It wouldn't have happened if I hadn't burned the sausages. That's why you had to leave him on the table."

Maybe there's some truth to that. It hadn't occurred to me.

"Alistair," Martin says. "You are not responsible for whatever happened to Dwayne."

That's what I should have said.

Esther gives Alistair a comforting squeeze on his shoulder.

That's what I should have done.

"I win!" Ruby says, waving her rod, with a tiny plastic fish attached, in everyone's face.

She looks at us expectantly, then quizzically, as if to ask what's the matter with us.

"Let's play again," Esther says. She resets the fish into the socket, straightens the game on the bed. Somehow those small orderly actions give me a sense that everything will work out.

Later in the day, there's a knock at the door. No one in the family has left the cabin since we returned from Fish Bowl. We haven't spoken specifically about what happened, but I suspect none of us wants to talk with Happy Sands residents other than Esther, who is with us. I have no answer for the question 'What happened?' And surely, that is what people want to know. I'm relieved when I open the door and see Sergeant Gardner, not a fellow renter. She also wants to know what happened, but at least she's working on the answer. And I'm relieved that Martin has opened the blinds and tidied up, making it easy for me to invite Sergeant Gardner into the cabin, rather than speak with her on the deck for all to see.

"First," she says, "Dwayne regained consciousness at the hospital. He seems to be doing fine."

"Thank goodness," I say.

"Second, we don't know much yet. He can't recall how he came to be on the floor beside the massage table. They are going to run more tests on him. We'll need you to file a statement. I'll wait while you fill out this form."

While I look for a pen she asks, "Do you know of anyone who might have wanted to hurt Dwayne?"

"Personally, I couldn't stand the guy," Martin says.

"Me neither," Alistair calls from his bedroom.

Not funny, I think. And not the right time to try to be funny.

Sergeant Gardner crosses her arms, says, "Disliking someone and wanting to hurt them are different things." Then she says to me, "Can I see the charts you've kept on Dwayne?"

"I don't keep charts here," I say.

"Oh," Sergeant Gardner says, raising her eyebrows. "No notes at all? Aren't you required to keep a record?"

"In theory," I say. "I'm on vacation here."

"Some vacation," Sergeant Gardner says.

Will she take the time to call the association that I am registered with? Report that I have not been following regulations? I hope she has bigger fish to fry.

After Sergeant Gardner leaves, we stay hunkered down in Rat's Nest. We all have a go at the fish game. Ruby continues to win. We watch shark shows and read all the Archie comics from the drawer under the coffee table. Esther goes home to Beehive. We eat grilled cheese sandwiches for dinner. Then popcorn. Then a bag of cookies. Martin, Alistair, and Ruby are better at dealing with our self-imposed, undiscussed, quarantine from the Happy Sands community. Perhaps they don't think of it as quarantine. Perhaps, to them, it is vacation time. Or family time. I, on the other hand, am increasingly both anxious and bored. I pace the inner perimeter of the cabin. Look in cupboards and drawers for no reason. Open the fridge. A drink would help me settle. A chill glass of Pinot. Yes, indeed. That's the ticket.

I place the bottle on the counter, twist off the cap. Pour myself a tumbler of wine. I'm not going to hide this glass of wine from anyone. After the day I've had, nobody can deny me this wine. I pick my glass off the counter and carry it to the couch, where I sit beside Martin.

"Thanks for your help today," I say.

"No problem," he says.

Then we sit quietly, and I slip back into the thoughts cycling through my head. What happened to Dwayne? Did I assume he was totally healthy because he's so buff? Because he is a MetaMan? Was I less observant because of the Red Eyes I drank, or was I just not paying attention?

I get up, refill my glass, sit back on the couch beside Martin.

He takes the glass out of my hand, sets it on the coffee table.

"I read the pamphlet on depression," Martin says. "I wish you'd just told me that you're feeling low. We should be able to talk."

Holy backfire. He thinks I gave him the pamphlet as a way of telling him that *I'm* depressed?

"How can I help you?" he asks.

"By giving me my glass of wine back," I say.

He hands me the glass of wine. "It's okay," he says, patting my thigh. "We'll work through this."

Work through what? I have so much going on in my head about Dwayne that I don't feel sure about anything. Martin doesn't seem depressed now. Maybe I am not as good at diagnosing people as I thought.

DAY 7

I don't swim this morning. I am on the Rat's Nest deck, sitting far back so I can see Cornflower Lake, but no one can see me. I'm still avoiding people, avoiding conversations about Dwayne. But I know the strategy can't last. And, sure enough, here comes Kathy.

"Hey, Ginny. What's up?" she asks. Like she doesn't know everything that is up.

"Hi," I say. I refrain from asking her if she wants a massage. Although, with my last client in the hospital, I'd like to see how she handles the response.

"Any news on Dwayne?" she asks.

"Last I heard he was doing all right."

"I'm thinking I should bake something for him. Take it to the hospital."

"That's an idea," I say.

"I'll bring Tara and Todd along. Might cheer him up."

Might not, I think.

"Do you want to come with us?" Kathy says.

Now that's an offer I didn't see coming. I'd like to see Dwayne. The last image I have of him is when he was wheeled into the ambulance. It would be good to see him conscious. It would be good to see him, period. But not with Kathy and her cake and her demon children.

I notice Sergeant Gardner walking towards us. Best to get rid of Kathy before the Sergeant arrives. There could be details I'd like to keep private. For instance, anything that connects Dwayne's hospitalization to my massage skills.

"Here comes someone I need to talk to," I say.

"Oh, the Mountie," Kathy says.

The Sergeant steps onto the deck. Looks at Kathy. Waits.

"I'll be on my way," Kathy finally says. As she passes the sergeant, she says to her, "Love the haircut."

Sergeant Gardner sits on the edge of a plastic chair near me.

"Since you are heading home tomorrow, I thought I'd tell you where this case is at."

I hold my breath.

"Dwayne suffered a toxic dose of anti-inflammatory muscle cream."

She doesn't seem like the type to joke around. And yet blaming muscle cream seems preposterous.

Sergeant Gardner reads my doubt, adds, "Methyl salicylate can be toxic. Especially if used on more than half the body."

"Dwayne used a lot of muscle cream," I say.

"The staff at the hospital noticed the smell right away."

"I never use that stuff on clients."

"No one's blaming you. Witnesses reported that he used it himself, by the bucket. And Dwayne says it is all his own doing. He was employing the more-is-better theory. But he's recovering quickly. He probably won't even have to miss the MetaMan race."

Sergeant Gardner presses her hands into her thighs and stands up.

"Gotta get back to work," she says. "Enjoy the rest of your vacation. Here's hoping I don't have to visit you or Happy Sands again this summer."

That's it? I feel like there should be more. What about the flamingoes? The boats? Shouldn't we have a drink together to seal our friendship? No, that would never happen. Sergeant Gardner seems happy to be rid of me.

"Do you know if Dwayne needs anything?" I ask. "Should I bring him anything from his cabin? Clothes? Toothbrush?"

120

"I'm sure his girlfriend will handle that."

His girlfriend. Of course, he has a girlfriend.

After Sergeant Gardner leaves, I think about walking to the fruit stand. Then I think about reading my book. The easiest choice would be to have a glass of wine, but even that seems like an effort. I close my eyes. I get bored. I open my eyes, spot a young woman on the other side of the property, checking out each cabin. She stops at Fish Bowl, knocks on the door, peers in. I recognize her Vancouver Canucks T-shirt. It's the woman from the Cinderella Laundromat. Today she is in tiny shorts instead of sweats, and by her legs I can tell she is an athlete. Probably a runner.

My spying on her is interrupted by Mrs. Edwards stomping up our deck. She has a plastic food storage container in her hands. And no brace around her neck.

Mrs. Edwards hands me the container. "Oatmeal cookies. For the drive home tomorrow," she says. "Sergeant Gardner told me you didn't hurt the flamingoes. She said they had a lead on a local kid, that it might take a while to complete the investigation. And they likely won't press charges."

"Did the same local kid untie the boats?"

"The sergeant said she has information that a different local kid untied the boats."

"Wow. What a neighbourhood," I say. I peel back the container's lid — the cookies look big and fabulous. This does not seem like the Mrs. Edwards I know. Maybe I have been missing her secret character. "Thank you," I say. And I mean it.

"You can keep the container." As she is walking away, she adds, "Esther tells me my neck issues are probably from using my e-reader."

Now, that is even better than cookies. I call after her, "Maybe Esther should be a massage therapist," I say.

Mrs. Edwards sends me a withering look. Okay, not a massage therapist.

The Cinderella woman, perhaps having noticed Mrs. Edwards talking to me, walks across the property, past the firepit, and towards me. She now has a gym bag.

"Hi," I say, when she is in front of our cabin. "I remember you from the car wash and laundromat?"

"Oh," she says. "I don't remember you. I'm looking for Ginny?"

Again, she forgets me? "You helped me get my skirt out of the vacuum."

"Oh right, I remember the skirt. Was that you?"

"Yes," I say.

"Awesome. I'm picking up some clothes for my boyfriend. Dwayne Champion. He's in the hospital. He said to tell you that he's sorry for any stress he caused you. He says you're the best massage therapist ever, and that he'll see you here next year."

"Tell him I wish him good luck in the MetaMan competition," I say. And I really do hope Dwayne Champion puts up his best possible time.

Martin, Alistair, Ruby, and I spend the afternoon at the beach. Martin has put on his swim trunks for the first time this vacation. He has coated his bared skin with a thick film of zinc-based sunscreen. There's a white clump of it behind his ear. And it looks like Ruby might have done the sloppy application on his back. There are small handprints pressed into the cream around his shoulders. Near his hip there is an etched happy face.

Alistair wears a T-shirt and his micro-mini bathing suit. It's the longest period of time his bare legs have been visible the whole holiday. Ruby, in the two-piece bathing suit she has lived in for a week, has found a peewee football on the beach. She creates competitive challenges for us: who can do the best dive into the water for the ball, throw the finest spiral, jump the highest out of the water to make an interception. She frequently appoints herself the winner. Mostly, though, we play casual catch while standing in the shallows.

I look around. Hey, this is nice. We have the beach almost to ourselves. Why couldn't the vacation have started this way? Why this scene only on the last day? The Roccos and Oliemens are out zipping around in their boats — but far enough out that they are not a distraction. Ruthanne and Dot float on their air mattresses. Like a couple of old otters, they hold hands to keep from drifting apart. Kathy and Tara and Todd must be at the hospital visiting Dwayne.

Esther joins us at the water for a bit. She hasn't gone so far as to put on shorts or a bathing suit, but she rolls up her pant legs and wades into the water. Alistair throws her the peewee football. She tosses it back to him, short, on purpose, so it hits the water and splashes him. A gentle water fight ensues between them, the purpose of which seems to be hugging each other.

Then Esther heads back to Beehive to help her mother string up some new chili pepper lights around the cabin. The flamingo replacement. I try not to judge the chili pepper lights. Okay, I can't stand them. What is this — a fiesta? But, to be fair, it seems sporting of Esther and Mrs. Edwards to go to the trouble of putting them up for one night. They leave tomorrow, too.

Late afternoon, we're still at the beach. Martin, Alistair, Ruby, and I swim out to the raft. Alistair runs off the diving board and cannonballs into the water. Ruby, with a hoot of delight, does the same. And then Martin, of all people, goes off the board and does a goofy jump. And it inspires me to think, go, Ginny, do a tinsica.

I walk most of the way down the board. After taking a few minutes to calm my nerves, I convince myself that I did so many tinsicas when I was young that the skill should still be in my muscle memory. I cartwheel my hands along the board and then, at the end of the board, I arch my back and twist as my feet come over my head and I glide into the water. A tinsica. In my mind, while I swim to the surface, the crowd goes wild, my life will be changed forever. I am now a sports celebrity. A Meta Woman.

But no. No one has seen my tinsica. Martin, Ruby, and Alistair are on the other side of the raft playing water tag. No problem. I shall perform my tinsica again. I climb the ladder onto the raft, walk onto the board. I call for my family's attention. I wait patiently for them to swim around to my side of the raft. They must witness my athleticism.

When the family is assembled and treading water, all eyes on me, I begin. My cartwheel is slower this time. Too slow. I contort myself to get my feet around. Not working. I contort more. Unlike my first tinsica off the board, I now feel like a forty-two-year-old woman wrenching her body into a teenage gymnastic move. I fall sideways into the water with a smack. And then my lower back spasms. I gasp and splash towards Martin, the nearest person floating in the water, and clutch him. He sputters, sinks almost entirely under water with my weight on him, then surfaces.

"Shore," is all I can say.

We are a flotilla. Everyone in a circle around me, helping me dog paddle through the water. It seems to take forever until my feet feel the bottom and I can walk, with some help from the shoulders of Martin and Alistair. Ruby, ahead of us, announces to all of Happy Sands that I hurt my back. I am in too much pain to be humiliated.

We make it to Rat's Nest. Martin helps me get out of my bathing suit and into my baby doll pajamas. He finds our first aid kit in the closet and zips it open. Moments later, he hands me a glass of water and some ibuprofen. If my back didn't hurt so much, I'd jump up and kiss him.

I stay in bed while my family makes dinner. I can hear them discussing what to make. There are options in the fridge.

If I felt better, I would make suggestions. Instead, I doze. Wake up in pain. Replay the failed tinsica in my mind. Doze again.

Eventually, they bring me dinner. Alistair enters the bedroom first with a tray. Ruby follows him with a glass of water. Martin is the last into the room. He carries a pillow from the other bedroom, presumably to help prop me up.

Alistair sets the tray on the bedside table. There's some sliced chicken on it. And a few vegetables. And a Summer Lovin' napkin.

"Beer can chicken," he says proudly.

"No barbecue fires were involved," Martin says. He puts an arm behind my shoulders, helps me sit up, stuffs the fresh pillow behind my back

"We know you like beer," Ruby says.

Beer can chicken — a whole chicken stuffed with a beer can and then barbecued — is a summer holiday favourite. I am sure it will taste excellent. But, alas, there goes my last beer.

Alistair steps away from the bedside table, and I notice his bright red legs.

"Alistair," I say, "your legs."

He shrugs. "I kind of got a sunburn today."

That's the understatement of the vacation. He is likely going to be asking for some of my ibuprofen. And that will be an opportunity for me. Ibuprofen in exchange for a promise that he will agree to a new bathing suit. I might be hurt, but I still have game.

Alistair and Martin lean against the bedroom wall while I start to eat. Ruby sits on the edge of my bed.

"You guys have already eaten?" I ask.

They nod.

"Why don't you go watch TV," I say. There's a sentence I never thought I'd say. Then again, I never thought I'd be eating beer can chicken in bed.

They don't move.

"What?" I ask.

Ruby says, "So, um, Mom, we have to tell you something."

I look at the kids, and at Martin. Everyone is so serious. What is this, an intervention? And why is that the first explanation that comes to mind?

Alistair says, "I untied the Rocco and Oliemen boats."

"Whatever for?" I ask.

"I felt bad for Ruby. I wanted her to get to play with Brie. And those guys never hire you. Well, not until Doug Oliemen came by."

A victimless crime, if you ask me. I don't say that to Alistair. I try to put a sage look on my face.

"And your role in it?" I ask Ruby.

"Different," Ruby says. "I beat up the flamingoes. With a badminton racquet. Mrs. Edwards shouldn't have blamed her sore neck on you."

Little Ruby. Little violent Ruby. I'm appalled and impressed. She did a lot of work on those flamingoes. Not just one broken neck, but several. Turns out those heavy badminton racquets were good for something. Flamingo murdering.

I look over at Martin. He does not seem remotely surprised by the news that our kids are the 'local kids' who did the pranks. They are the Happy Sands pranksters. And by pranksters, I mean delinquents.

"You knew?" I ask Martin.

He shrugs, says, "You were," he pauses, searching for a word, "busy."

I will have to tell Sergeant Gardner. That's the right move. That's better than trying to pack up this instant, donning wigs and stick-on moustaches, and speeding back to Alberta. Still, it's embarrassing that just when Sergeant Gardner is finally done with me, she'll have to come out here to deal with my kids. And what would dealing with my kids involve? What sort of heavy-handed 'lesson' would they have to learn? I try to change positions, adjust the pillows. My back hurts, and I'm on painkillers — what better excuse could there be to not contact Sergeant Gardner? Yes. That's it. I'm hurt, not myself. That's my story, and I'm sticking to it.

Martin comes over to the bed to help me roll onto my side. And as though he read my mind, he whispers, "I told Sergeant Gardner. She said it's good we are leaving Happy Sands tomorrow."

All is well. Or well enough. For now. I feel sleepy, from revelations, resolution and pain. And too many ibuprofen tablets. Alistair, Ruby, and Martin are still in the room. I wish they would leave. Stop hovering.

Martin picks up my plate from the bedside table, ushers the kids out of the bedroom. A sudden question clutches at my heart. All has not been solved.

"Wait," I say. Perhaps because of all the pillows they have propped under my head, which have slightly constricted my windpipe, it comes out as a stage whisper, the dramatic voice of a deathbed scene.

They stop, turn. I must ask them. No time like the present.

"What about the penis on the sand version of Moby Trout?" I ask.

"Oh, we heard that was the old ladies, Dot and Ruthanne," Alistair says.

Case closed.

I nap, really nap, for about an hour. When I wake up, I hear someone in the kitchen doing the dishes. It's a lovely sound. I listen for a few moments, enjoying the sound of the tap rinse, and the clunk of a dish going into the drying rack. But I want to get up. It's our last night of vacation. I shift my feet to the floor, use the bed for support as I work my way to the bedroom door.

"Oh, hello," Martin says from the kitchen sink when I open the bedroom door. "I thought you'd be out for the night. The kids have gone for a swim."

"Want to sit outside?" I ask.

"Those chairs on the deck won't be good for your back," Martin says.

"I know. But I want to see the lake."

Martin and I make it onto the deck in time to see Alistair and Ruby walking up from the beach, returning from their last swim of the holiday. Alistair carries a plastic chaise lounge on his head. Ruby, wrapped in a towel, the tail of it dragging in the sand, skips along beside him.

Just before they reach the deck, Alistair dumps the lounger on the ground, beside the one that I used when Ruby and Brie were sleeping on our deck. He sits on the edge of the lounger, looks towards Beehive, for Esther, I presume. Ruby spreads her towel on my old lounger, lies face down, arms dangling, fingers stirring the sand.

Martin serves cubes of melon to everyone, plus a glass of water for me. What I'd like is a glass of Pinot. But it seems everyone here is happier if I don't drink booze. I will be a family-pleasing teetotaler, mainly because it would hurt too much to get out of the chair and pour myself a drink.

"Why don't you quit staring at Beehive and go get Esther?" Ruby says to Alistair.

"It's not that easy," Alistair says.

"I'll go do it," Ruby says. She pushes off her chair and moves her arms as though she is going to start jogging to Beehive.

"No way," Alistair says. And he's out of his lounger, running towards Beehive, shirtless, in a teeny bathing suit, with sun burned thighs.

In no time, Alistair and Esther are back. Esther in her full coverage and Alistair practically nude. They sit together on the lounger, awkwardly, there is not room for two side-by-side butts in those chairs, even two young teenage butts, but it is cute, in a dumb-young-love way.

We sit in peace. Waves from Cornflower Lake ripple into the beach. Clouds roll across the rising moon, creating another dark night. But not all dark — Mrs. Edward's new chili peppers are lighting Happy Sands. Certainly not creating a fiesta atmosphere, but the chili lights are vacation-y, in a junky bar kind of way.

Early tomorrow, we will drive home. Slowly — because Martin will be behind the wheel. My back won't allow me to drive. We will not be visiting any drive-thrus. Martin, who seems downright excited about the trip home, has announced that we will stop and get out of the car and eat inside a restaurant. He also has us stopping at the Rogers Pass historical site. He alleges these stops are for my back health, so I can get out of the car and do gentle movements, small stretches. We'll take our time, he assures me. More like we'll waste our time, I think.

I have already offered Alistair the front passenger seat for the trip home because, with his sunburn, he'll need room to extend his legs as much as possible. The fewer surfaces those bright red sticks touch, the better. Unlike me, Alistair will be able to go to work on Monday. Standing at the gas station cash register won't irritate his burn. Me, on the other hand, well, it will be weeks before I can go back to Prairie Physiotherapy. Massage is a physical job. I can't do it with this injury.

Ruby and I will sit in the back seat tomorrow, my massage table between us. Sergeant Gardner said we could take the table from the Fish Bowl deck, and Martin loaded it into its travel case and then into the car. Ruby might still be wearing her bathing suit tomorrow. She will probably sleep in it tonight, and then why change for the drive home? More importantly, Ruby has offered to read aloud to me from her dragon book. I have become the child, and everyone else in the car has somehow become my parent.

Which is all to say, the trip home will be horrible. And at the same time, like the whole holiday, perfect. That is, for a family vacation. We might not have seen Moby Trout. But we came close.

ACKNOWLEDGEMENTS

This is a short book that took a long time to complete. A seed story for this novella was published in my 2012 collection *Western Taxidermy*, but I was mulling over a "summer story" or "beach read" long before that publication. Drafts have been on my computer, usually in a virtual drawer, for so many years that I have certainly forgotten many of the people who helped along the way. Apologies to those I fail to mention here. I do remember, and am thankful for, early feedback from Vivian Hansen and Betty Jane Hegerat.

More recently, I owe thanks to Joan Dixon for tireless insightful edits. And thanks also to RMTs Deanna McDevitt at Threepoint Massage Therapy and Keith Morrison at Cascadia Therapeutics for massage factchecks and input. Any creative license, misinformation, or straight-up errors with regard to massage therapy are entirely my own doing.

This book would not exist without the fine work of the University of Calgary Press. Thanks to all you Brave and Brilliant people for your expertise and for publishing novellas. Special gratitude to editor Aritha van Herk for her wise comments and perceptive questions, and for bringing a sense of fun back to the process. Kudos to copyeditor Naomi K. Lewis for the final tow to the finish line.

Love and appreciation to Mike, Ross, and Stuart for past summer vacations, and for not being the family in this story.

—b

Barb Howard is the author of *Notes for Monday*, *Whipstock*, *The Dewpoint Show*, and the award-winning short story collection *Western Taxidermy*. She has served as President of the Writers' Guild of Alberta, Writer-in-Residence at the Calgary Public Library, and editor of Freefall Magazine, and has taught Creative Writing at the University of Calgary, the Alexandra Writers' Centre, and the Banff Centre. Barb is the Calgary writing mentor for The Shoe Project, a literary and performance workshop for immigrant women, and sits on its board of directors. She is also a member of the board of directors for Calgary Arts Development and the Calgary Arts Foundation. She lives in Calgary, Alberta.

BRAVE & BRILLIANT SERIES

SERIES EDITOR:
Aritha van Herk, Professor, English, University of Calgary
ISSN 2371-7238 (PRINT) ISSN 2371-7246 (ONLINE)

Brave & Brilliant encompasses fiction, poetry, and everything in between and beyond. Bold and lively, each with its own strong and unique voice, Brave & Brilliant books entertain and engage readers with fresh and energetic approaches to storytelling and verse.